Tears of a Cherry Blossom Tree

By

Author: Fletcher Johnson Jr.

Publisher:

Tears of a Cherry Blossom Tree

This story takes place during the spring of 1908 in a small, yet steadily growing town located in Central Georgia. Because of its commemorative Cherry Blossom trees that bloom every spring, the town carries the proud distinction of being "The Cherry Blossom Capital of the World." The events unfold at Stillwaters, a newly built orphanage lovingly owned and ran by "The Lady in Pink." Stillwaters, surrounded by the Cherry Blossom trees that give this orphanage of "peace" such divine significance, triumphantly lives up to its name for all its occupants entering its dwelling.

Tears of a Cherry Blossom Tree

This is a work of fiction. Names, characters, places, and incidents either are the product of the author's imagination or are used fictitiously. Any resemblance to actual persons, living or dead, events, or locales is entirely coincidental.

Copyright © 2018 by Fletcher Johnson Jr.

All rights reserved. No part of this book may be reproduced or used in any manner without written permission of the copyright owner except for the use of quotations in a book review. For more information, address: info@piercingfocus.com.

First printing edition 2018

First Published by *Piercing Focus LLC 12/01/2018*

Book design by *Piercing Focus LLC*

Map by *Piercing Focus LLC*

ISBN 978-1-7325238-1-4 (Paperback)

Library of Congress Control Number: 1-7174568875

www.divinedovecalls.com

Publishing Company: *Piercing Focus LLC*

Author: *Fletcher Johnson Jr.*

Editor: *Piercing Focus LLC*

Illustrator: *Piercing Focus LLC*

Tears of a Cherry Blossom Tree

DEDICATION

I would like to dedicate this book to my sweet, beautiful late mother, Annie Pearl Johnson, the real "Lady in Pink." Your genuine, precious heart and overwhelming loving kindness towards others made me the loving, caring husband, father, and friend that I am today. I love and miss you!

ACKNOWLEDGEMENT

"I want to thank my beautiful wife, Valerie, and my three wonderful sons, Jarvis, my firstborn and inspiration, Christopher, my middle son and scholar, and Joshua, my youngest and creative artist. You bring so much joy to my life. To my wonderful daughter-in-law, Jennifer. You are a precious gift to our son [Jarvis] and family. To my Goddaughter, Ke'Asia, thank you for being a special daughter. A special thank you to my pastor and the Ingleside Baptist church family. To my brothers, Ricky, Roy, Marcus, Darrell and Fred, I love you all. To my God-sisters, Renae Jefferson and the late Rev. Amanda Jefferson, I love you both. To my adopted mothers, Dr. Barbara Thompson, Betty Hill, the late Priscilla Martin and the late Janie Mays, I love you all. To my very talented illustrator, the late Mary Norwick, who toured and signed alongside me during our first book release, I will always cherish you and our memories. To Sussana, Arabella, Harrison, Richard, Olympia, Kaitlyn, Meghan, Tonyour, Joe, Nathan, Camila, Natalie, Amy, Laura, Brenda, Leah, Will, Barbara, Tywanna, Oscar Lee, Eric, Alfreda, Rob, Sheila, Michelle, Connie, Larry, and others, thanks for your friendship. To my late cousin, Gladys Evans, who presided over my wedding, we love and miss you. To my late cousin, Reginald Poole, and Baby (Bo), we will never stop loving and missing you all."

(Author, Fletcher Johnson Jr.)

PREFACE

Tears of a Cherry Blossom Tree

Readers can expect to feel a sense of adoration, empathy, and awe when accounting the dramatic lives of former orphans and their adoptive families who faced traumatic events and endured fears of uncertainty until they each reached the end of their own climactic journey. Even though it is a fictional account, this book parallels the unselfish life and devotion of my late mother, Annie Pearl Johnson, in bringing hope to neglected and displaced children and families. This book also pays tribute to social service agencies that provide loving foster and adoptive parents for children who have been displaced, neglected, abused and abandoned. It is a book for all ages.

Background of Stillwaters' Characters

1. Caroline Saxon: Her mother passed away, leaving her with no place to go. Lovingly adopted by Betty and Jim, a couple from New York.

2. Katherine Clemons: Her Grandmother passed away, leaving her with no place to go. Lovingly adopted by Maam Kizi and her family from Africa.

3. Victoria Simmons: Her father was killed in the line of duty and received a Purple Heart for bravery. She had no other family and no place to live other than Stillwaters. Adopted by a loving family from Japan.

4. Marilyn Clisby: She was emotionally and physically abused as a child. Lovingly adopted by Maria from Georgia.

5. Reba Alderman: She was physically abused as a young girl and taken away by the state. Adopted by a loving family from France. The Lady in Pink: She owned and operated Stillwaters' Orphanage.

SUMMARY

This story takes place during the spring of 1908 in a small, yet steadily growing town located in Central Georgia. Because of its commemorative Cherry Blossom trees that bloom every spring, the town carries the proud distinction of being "The Cherry Blossom Capital of the World." The events unfold at Stillwaters, a newly built orphanage lovingly owned and ran by "The Lady in Pink." Stillwaters, surrounded by the Cherry Blossom trees that give this orphanage of "peace" such divine significance, triumphantly lives up to its name for all its occupants entering its dwelling.

CONTENTS

Dedication v
Acknowledgement vi
Preface vii
Prologue xi

Part I: *Precious Serenity*
Chapter One Stillwaters' Haven 2
Chapter Two Bonjour, Dear Friends! 22
Chapter Three Namesake Carvings 32
Chapter Four Homeward Bound For Africa 55

Part II: Journeys
Chapter Five Devastating News At Stillwaters 96
Chapter Six The Diagnosis 122
Chapter Seven The Manifestation 154
Chapter Eight The Standoff 166
Chapter Nine Kobe's Horse Goes Missing! 170
The Lady In Pink's Last Letter 229
About The Author 231
References 234

PROLOGUE

*W*hile excitedly awaiting the arrival of five little girls to her newly established orphanage in 1908, "Stillwaters", The Lady in Pink, sitting in her Livingroom rocking chair, resumes reading the letter from the nearby Georgia agency that beforehand, screened and selected prospective parents seeking to adopt. She looks over the list carefully while praying to God that the agency made the right decisions in its selections. "Lord knows that these precious babies have been through enough," sighs The Lady in Pink. As she browses through the girls' background history report, she discovers Victoria Simmons is age 5 with black hair, brown eyes and lost her father in a war; Katherine Clemons is age 6 with rose-golden hair, blue eyes and lost her grandmother; Caroline Saxon is age 7 with brunette hair, green eyes and lost her mother; Marilyn Clisby is age 6 with strawberry-blonde hair, gray eyes, emotionally, verbally and physically abused, and taken away from her abusive mother. Reba Alderman is age 9 with red hair, hazel eyes, abandoned by her mother, physically abused, and was taken away from her abusive stepfather. Three of the girls were due to arrive on Day One and the other two girls were to arrive on Day Two. The Lady in Pink understands the pain these young children have faced. At age 30 and the sole survivor of her family, she knows they are scared and lonely and in need of lots of warm muffins. She feels the emptiness of her seven-bedroom home and knows she is doing the right thing. Who needs all this space to themselves anyways? She smiles, thinking about her mother. It is only fitting that she carries on the tradition of welcoming the lost and lonely into her home.

Shortly, she hears the screech of tires halting on the gravel. She peeks out the window and quickly puts the letter away in the pocket of her apron. After giving her apron a quick pat, she quickly smooths the sides of her honey-brown hair, pins it up in a loose bun, and rushes to the door. Then, adding a quick prayer, The Lady in Pink exuberantly opens the door with a wide, beaming smile framed on her gentle, slim face and cheerfully exclaims, "Welcome to Stillwaters!"

PART I:

PRECIOUS SERENITY

⁴ One generation passeth away, and another generation cometh: but the earth abideth forever.

⁵ The sun also ariseth, and the sun goeth down, and hasteth to his place where he arose.

(Ecclesiastes 1:4-5, KJV)

CHAPTER ONE

STILLWATERS' HAVEN

Being the first to arrive on Day One at Stillwaters' Orphanage, a little girl by the name of Caroline Saxon made it clear that she was furious and confused, pulling at her soft brunette hair and screaming, "I want to go home! Where is mama?!"

The caretaker smiled at the confused little girl and sat quietly in her rocking chair. She then began calmly rocking back and forth and gently explained, "She was carried away by angels, but one day you will see her again. Why don't you come sit with me?"

Caroline turned her big green eyes up to the caretaker, who was wearing a pink flowered dress. She contemplated for a moment whether she should trust her. Hesitantly, Caroline wiped the tears from her cheeks and slowly climbed into the smiling woman's arms. "What's your name?" the girl asked.

"Well, you know, I really love wearing pink dresses, since I was about your age actually. You may simply call me *The Lady in Pink*. Do you like it?"

Caroline shrugged her shoulders, unsure how she felt about the caretaker's name, and then said, "The Lady in Pink? My name is Caroline and mama wouldn't wake up to give me breakfast. I shook her like this." Caroline placed her little hand on The Lady in Pink's arm and started shaking it to reenact the scene with her mother. The little girl then said, "She still wouldn't wake up. I went outside and screamed, and the neighbor lady came. Mama never opened her eyes and a doctor came and took her away. Can you go help them?" Caroline looked down as she spoke.

"Well, Sweetie, she's awake in a beautiful place now—in the sky," replied The Lady.

"Let's go there. She forgot to take me with her."

"In time, my dear. In time. Where is your father or papa?" The Lady asked.

"I don't have a papa."

"Do you have any brothers or sisters?"

"No, it's just me and mama. She said she was going to get me a new dress for my 8th birthday. Maybe she will come back then?" pondered Caroline.

A silent hush and the soothing sound of the creaking rocking chair filled the room for a few hours. As Caroline rocked back and forth in the arms of The Lady in Pink, an unexpected loud knock was heard at the front door. Immediately, the little girl leaped down from the arms of The Lady and rushed to the door. "It's her! Mama is knocking at the door! Mama! Open the door, Lady in Pink! I'm here, Mama! I knew you would come back for me," rejoiced Caroline.

The Lady in Pink rushed behind Caroline, gently moving her out of the doorway to open the door. The Lady in Pink greeted a tall gentleman in a gray suit, holding a blue-eyed little girl's hand on his right, and papers in his left. When the gentleman handed the papers to The Lady in Pink to sign for the child, she noticed the name of the little girl in the letter was Katherine Clemons. The Lady escorted her inside the orphanage. "I want my Granny! Come get me, Granny! Please don't leave me. No!" shouted Katherine in a high-pitched, squeaky tone.

Tears of a Cherry Blossom Tree

The Lady in Pink cuddled Katherine and caressed her rose-golden hair. "It's going to be alright. Your grandmother is in a beautiful place in the sky."

"Why is she in the sky? Can we go and get her down?" Katherine then looked up at the ceiling, trying to understand *how* and *why* her grandmother was in the sky. "My granny fell in the flower garden. Her eyes were open, but she didn't get up when I called her name… Why didn't she get up?" questioned Katherine.

"Dear, she is tending to a more beautiful garden now. She is healthy and happy and waiting for you. One day you will see her there. But, until then, wonderful people will take very good care of you and love you as their own child. I promise." The Lady assured to Katherine. "Do you have any brothers, sisters, or a papa?"

"Um, just Granny," Katherine sadly replied to the caretaker.

"She's with my mama and they are together," Caroline told Katherine. When Katherine made eye contact with Caroline, she stared at her with confusion. "My name is Caroline, and my mama wouldn't wake up either." Katherine furiously got down from The Lady in Pink's arms and frightfully stood doe-eyed in the corner. Caroline then walked timidly over towards Katherine, tapped her on the shoulder and whispered, "It's going to be okay, that's what The Lady in Pink said."

Then, she gave Katherine a gentle hug and softly cried, drenching both of their dresses with warm, salty tears. After a moment, they sat down on the hardwood floor and, without saying a word, both nodded off to sleep in the corner. About two hours later, Caroline and Katherine woke up from their nap; they were startled by a little voice angrily shouting from the front entrance.

"Let go of my hand, Lady! You Pink Twiddle Bug! You Pink Skittle Bug! I want my Papa! My Papa is coming back from the war to get me! He is not dead! Stop saying that! Stop pulling my arm, Lady! Let go of me! I...want...my...Papa!" shouted the unknown voice. The Lady in Pink gently pulled in the angry small girl by the name of Victoria Simmons inside the orphanage, while lovingly removing her hat. Once The Lady coaxed Victoria inside and closed the door, the black-haired little girl stood in the middle of the room with a mean frown on her face, glaring at everyone with angry brown eyes. The other two girls motioned for her to come over to sit down beside them. Victoria crossed both of her arms and defiantly stomped as hard as she could while walking over to sit with the other girls.

"Stop looking at me! You both have Roly Poly eyes!" Victoria angrily shouted.

The Lady gently reprimanded, "I know you're scared, but that wasn't a nice thing to say to your new friends. They're also scared."

Victoria looked down at the floor, visibly shaking with anger. "I am mad, and they are not my friends. I want my Papa and don't want to be here. Where is my Papa?!"

The Lady went and sat down in her rocking chair, extending her hands to Victoria.

"I'm not going to sit in your lap! You're not my Papa! Lady!" shouted Victoria, defiantly.

She ran towards the front door, frantically grabbed the doorknob, and quickly escaped through the neat row of bushes that framed the front porch. The Lady, along with the other girls, followed Victoria outside where they found her crying underneath the Cherry Blossom Tree for her father. Blossoms began falling on her head just as Victoria's tears fell onto her dress. They all gathered around her to console Victoria.

"What's your name, sweetie?" The Lady asked politely.

"Victoria, and my Papa was in a war. He promised he would come back for me, but a man said Papa wasn't coming back. I don't believe that mean man."

"Where is your mother, brothers and sisters?"

"Papa said mama died when I was really little, and I don't have brothers. I don't have sisters either," Victoria said.

"How old are you?" Katherine asked.

"Five," responded Victoria.

As Victoria calmed down, she began to playfully shuffle the pink blossoms on the ground where she was kneeling. Everyone joined in by delicately throwing blossoms on each other's heads, timidly smiling.

"Let's go inside and I will bake everyone Cherry Blossom Cream Cheese Muffins. How does that sound?" The Lady asked.

The girls looked at each other gingerly with slight grins. They all joined hands while entering the orphanage and into the kitchen area. As they sat at the kitchen table, The Lady in Pink began reaching for and calling out the recipe ingredients.

"This is my late mother's, Ada Bell Poole's, Cherry Blossom famous Cream Cheese Muffin recipe and I am going to add the following ingredients: 6 cups of flour." "Like the ones in the dirt?" asked Caroline." The Lady chuckled and continued, "2 cups, sugar." Victoria interjected, "Sugar, yummy!" The Lady went on, "1 teaspoon of cinnamon." "Oh, cinnamon! I love it," Katherine said. "You girls aren't going to make this easy for me, are you?" The Lady laughed. The girls smiled and giggled at their caretaker.

After The Lady in Pink gathered the rest of the ingredients to make the muffins, Katherine asked, "Hey…What do you mean by *late mother*? She didn't come home on time?"

"It means that my mother is no longer with me. She is in heaven."

"Where is heaven?" Caroline asked.

"It's a beautiful place above the clouds where we all hope to join our family members again," answered The Lady with a warm smile. The caretaker then said, "Now, girls, I'm going to give each of you a chore. These are the directions that I want each of you to follow in helping me prepare the muffins. First, Victoria, in this large bowl, I want you to take this sifter and sift the flour, sugar, baking powder and cinnamon together."

"Kay, Pink Lady," responded Victoria loudly. The Lady in Pink clasped her hand over her mouth trying to refrain from bursting out in laughter.

"It's The Lady in Pink! Not Pink Lady, Victoria!" yelled Katherine in defense of The Lady.

"Katherine, it's not nice to yell at Victoria or anyone for that matter. Please apologize," gently rebuked The Lady.

"I'm sorry," mumbled Katherine shyly.

The Lady in Pink looked at Katherine, smiled and said, "It's quite alright dear and thank you for apologizing." She then looked around the kitchen and continued, "Hmm, let's see, where was I? Oh, Caroline, in this bowl, you will help me cream together the butter, eggs, milk and almonds."

"Okay," replied Caroline.

"Katherine, you can help me mix the butter into the ingredients," instructed The Lady.

"Yes, Ma'am."

"Everyone can help me stir in the cream cheese and then the cherries. I am going to fill the pan and sprinkle the tops with cinnamon and put everything in the oven for 15-20 minutes. Once we take it out of the oven and let it cool down a bit, we can top the muffins with pink icing."

"Making muffins is fun," Caroline said.

As the girls sifted and stirred the ingredients, flour, cream cheese and icing were all in their hair and on their dresses.

"Can we lick the bowl and spoon?" Victoria asked eagerly.

"Why, yes, enjoy," answered The Lady as she stirred hot wood chips inside of the black, potbelly stove.

The girls all joined in by licking the bowls and spoons. Later, the muffins were ready.

"Okay, girls, it's time for icing. Victoria, you can help me spread the icing while Katherine and Caroline tidy up," The Lady said. "Now I need a spreader," she continued.

"This is so much fun!" shouted Victoria. The Lady smiled and listened to sounds of laughter as they spread the icing. After everyone completed their duties in the kitchen, The Lady in Pink made an announcement, "Okay, children, we are all done and it's time to eat. Girls, please take a seat." Following the caretaker's instructions, Victoria, Katherine and Caroline eagerly took a seat at the kitchen table. The Lady prayed and blessed the dessert treats. "I want you all to know that even though this is a hard time for you, please feel free to share your feelings," The Lady said.

Victoria, with a mouth full of muffin, garbled, "I want my Papa."

"My granny is supposed to come back for me," sadly stated Katherine while staring down at her plate.

Caroline then asked, "Can you wake up mama, so I can see her again, Lady in Pink?"

The Lady remained silent; she was overwhelmed with sorrow for the girls. "You know, girls, I felt lonely and afraid when my mother died. It's okay to cry when you're sad. I cried too."

"Where did you go when your mama died?" Katherine asked.

"Well, I stayed with my aunt, my mother's sister, until I was an adult. But when my mother was alive, she would take in little children who had no place to go, like you, girls. After my mother went up to the sky, I promised her that I would take care of little children as she did. So, I decided to make my home an orphanage for children who needed a safe place." The Lady in Pink then looked up and sighed, "I truly miss the sound of my mother's voice, especially when she read books to me."

"Can you read a book to us?" Caroline asked.

"Of course! As soon as everyone finishes eating."

After dessert, they all entered the living room. While the girls sat quietly on the floor, The Lady grabbed a book from a beautiful, antique bookshelf and sat in her rocking chair, facing the girls. Minutes after she began reading, the soft sound of her voice lulled the girls off to sleep. The Lady smiled and stared longingly at the sleeping girls. The caretaker noticed how peaceful the little orphans looked as they slept on the floor with their arms clutching their quilt-patched dolls. She didn't want to awaken them but after allowing them to sleep a little while longer, she nudged them gently and settled the little orphaned girls in for their first night at Stillwaters. Feeling very exhausted, The Lady retired to her own bedroom and, after saying special prayers for each child, immediately dozed off to sleep.

    During the morning hours of Day Two, the orphans were all in the bathroom taking refreshing hot baths in a tin tub. After bathing, the little girls excitedly put on clean dresses donated from the local mission, which were washed, pressed, and folded beforehand by The Lady in Pink. She then prepared a hot breakfast for everyone, while making sure to put aside extra food for the other expected orphans seen in her paperwork. Unexpectedly, a loud car horn and siren sounded outside the window. The Lady in Pink peeked through the curtain and hurriedly stepped outside while the girls ate. Moments later, she came back inside holding a sleeping girl. Everyone could tell that she had been previously crying by the tear streaks on her cheeks and her still wet lace collar of her worn, thin dress. There were noticeable bruises and scratches on both her arms and legs, as well as what appeared to be deep rope burns on both her wrists. The girls left the breakfast table, peeked outside the window and quietly observed a black and white car with a red light and loud siren driving away. The girls then followed The Lady as she carried the battered, strawberry-blonde haired child to a bedroom and gently placed her on a bed.

"This is your new friend. Her name is Marilyn Clisby and she's 6-years-old. We're going to take good care of her," said The Lady in tears. The curious girls watched the injured newcomer for a long time and then quietly climbed into bed alongside her. They all gently embraced Marilyn and emitted soft, sweet words into her ears until they too fell asleep. Looking on at the precious sight, The Lady sighed sympathetically—her little visitors were all tired from their long, traumatic journeys. The Lady left the room and quietly wept. "I cannot believe a mother could do such a thing," she finally stated indignantly, while shaking her head and wiping her teary eyes with her apron.

Hours later, Marilyn woke up along with the other girls. "Please, don't take me back."

"What's your name?" Victoria asked.

With fearful gray eyes and her right thumb in her mouth, the injured newcomer replied in a faint voice, "Marilyn."

"Did you fall and get hurt?" Katherine asked.

"No. Mama hurt me," cried Marilyn.

The Lady suddenly heard crying and ran into the room. "No! Get away from me! Please don't hit me," cried Marilyn as she crouched in the corner of the room, tightly closing her eyes.

The Lady in Pink motioned to the other girls to back away from Marilyn. The Lady slowly moved in closer to Marilyn, being mindful not to frighten her and softly said, "I promise that no one here will hurt you. I am going to take good care of you. Darling, please tell me, do you have brothers or sisters?" The frightened girl shook her head no, with her head down.

"How about a father or papa," asked The Lady

Marilyn shook her head no again and then looked up at The Lady and whispered, "Mama said he left 'cause of me."

"Sweetie, it's not your fault. You are just a child," The Lady explained.

"Mama said it is my fault and calls me bad names. She calls me ugly and um—stupid. Mama always tells me that she hates me and hopes I die," Marilyn said, pointing at the bruises and dried blood on her body. "She tried to do it yesterday."

"Sweetie, I will never hurt or call you bad names." With both hands extended with love, The Lady beckoned Marilyn. "Please come here and let me give you a hug."

Marilyn sensed an unfamiliar feeling of trust as she stared into The Lady in Pink's loving, light brown eyes but still didn't move from the corner. "I have an idea, how about I make you some delicious breakfast. Marilyn, would you like that?" The Lady asked, cautiously reaching out her hand toward the scared child. Marilyn slowly moved her head up and down and timidly grabbed the caretaker's hand. The Lady gently led Marilyn into the kitchen. As the caretaker prepared a breakfast plate for Marilyn, the girls all sat down beside her.

"I like the biscuits and syrup. Can I have more?" Marilyn asked.

"Of course, I have more than enough," The Lady said, hearing the smacking and chomping sounds resonate throughout the kitchen as Marilyn devoured her meal.

The girls all looked on in silent amazement while staring at the rapid pace of Marilyn's eating and drinking mannerisms. "I bet that I can eat faster than you," Katherine said.

"No, girls, we don't race during breakfast. We use our best table manners. It's okay Marilyn, you can slow down and take your time. I don't want you to choke on your breakfast," The Lady explained with concern.

"I eat like this all the time because mama doesn't feed me every day," Marilyn said.

The Lady was heart-broken for the abused girl, she then said to the orphans, "Excuse me, girls, I believe I forgot something in my room. I'll be back shortly, so behave." The caretaker dashed into her bedroom, closing the door behind her. Seconds later, sounds of weeping could be heard coming from The Lady in Pink's bedroom.

Victoria got up from the kitchen table and walked over to The Lady's door. "Are you hurt? Why are you crying, Lady in Pink?" Victoria asked.

The Lady in Pink opened the door and hugged Victoria with tears streaming down her face. She then walked back to the kitchen and kissed Marilyn on the cheek. "You can eat as many times as you would like. I even have some leftover muffins for dessert."

Marilyn climbed up in the chair and kissed The Lady on her cheek before getting down to finish her breakfast. The other girls smiled as they looked on.

Later in the day, the girls all sat in the living room listening to The Lady's favorite songs on the phonograph. "I loved baseball as a child. As a little girl, I enjoyed singing the baseball song with my father when we attended local games. Let me play it for you and when we get to the chorus, *'Take me out to the ball game',* you little ladies can join in," The Lady said. As the music began playing, The Lady sang the chorus line and the girls sung along.

Tears of a Cherry Blossom Tree

Moments later, they heard a knock at the door. The Lady stopped singing, looked at the girls and instructed, "Stay put children, I will return soon." She then headed towards the door.

After The Lady in Pink left the living room, the orphans all stared at each other in silence until Katherine excitedly blurted out to the group, "Maybe it's one of our parents! Maybe one of them came back from that beautiful place The Lady told us about!"

"I knew my papa would come back!" shouted Victoria.

"I hope it's not mama," Marilyn sighed.

The other girls quickly turned their attention to Marilyn, looking upon her with sorrow. Seconds later, The Lady in Pink returned holding the hand of a new little red-haired girl. "Everyone, this is Reb—" The Lady's sentence was cut short as the fiery, red-haired girl unexpectantly started singing from the top of her lungs,

"Up and down we go, hopping on the floor, spin around and touch the ground, stand up and touch your nose." While singing, the little visitor quickly released her hand from The Lady in Pink's grasp and started skipping from the living room to the kitchen and throughout the house, starting to sing another song, *"I'm Free! I'm Free! No more tears, no more sadness, no more fear, and no more madness!"* The girls began to smile at that happy red-haired visitor, but quickly burrowed their brow with confusion when they noticed old and fresh bruises and

scars on her legs and arms—just like Marilyn. No one dared to ask her what had happened, as it was a visible sign of abuse of some sort. Although she appeared to be happy and relieved, they could still tell that she was scared and hurting. As the red-haired girl calmed down and circled back to everyone, Marilyn asked, "What is your name?"

"Reba Alderman and I'm 9 ½ years old," she replied.

The Lady in Pink then guided her into the kitchen to have a private moment with her. "Darling, I am so glad you're here. You seem quite cheerful."

"Yeah, because I don't have to worry about my stepfather anymore. He can no longer hurt me!" celebrated Reba.

"I am so sorry about what happened to you, sweetie. I promise that you will be safe from harm here. Where's your mother?" The Lady asked.

"She left me with my stepfather and never came back for me."

"Darling, what about your father, brothers and sisters?"

"I never met my real father. My mother told me that he worked on the railroad. I have no brothers or sisters," Reba said.

"Darling, you now have me and several friends that are going to be kind to you. Let's get you some breakfast."

The Lady prepared breakfast for Reba and sat with her as she completed her meal. Moments later, Reba ran into the living room where the girls were all sitting and playing on the floor.

Marilyn then quietly retreated from the rest of the girls and sneaked inside The Lady in Pink's room to get some soothing ointment from the mahogany chest of drawers. She returned to the group, took Reba by the hand, and led her to The Lady in Pink's room. Upon entering the room, Marilyn motioned for Reba to sit on the edge of the bed. Reba looked confused by the gesture at first, but obeyed Marilyn's request and sat down. The rest of the girls followed her and intently watched Marilyn as she rubbed the ointment on Reba's scars and bruises. "This was done to me too," Marilyn said in a comforting tone while blinking away tears.

Reba knowingly nodded her head, then repeated her song with cadence—quieter this time. The girls laughed and giggled as they joined in and rehearsed the rhythmic lines.

The Lady in Pink curiously peeked inside the room and smiled as she watched them bond. Marilyn got off the bed and found The Lady standing outside her bedroom door, observing them.

Tears of a Cherry Blossom Tree

There was a knock at the front door and The Lady went to open it. After she opened the door, she looked around and didn't see anyone, but noticed a large envelope on the porch. When The Lady in Pink picked up the envelope and opened it, she noticed there were adoption letters inside for each of the girls.

Marilyn walked up to The Lady and sweetly asked her, "May we go outside?"

"Of course!" replied The Lady. The girls joined hands like old friends and ran outside to play games underneath the Cherry Blossom Tree with pink blossoms gently falling on each of the girls' heads as they fluffed them in the air. The Lady walked outside to witness the beautiful scene of the orphan girls playing around Cherry Blossom Tree. She clasped both her hands to her heart in silence, cherishing the moment, for The Lady knew separation would soon come. As she turned to walk back into the house, a beautiful white dove, with satin wings swooped down by her and took off again. The Lady simply smiled and continued back into the house to prepare dinner.

CHAPTER TWO

BONJOUR, DEAR FRIENDS!

As The Lady prepared dinner, she occasionally peeked out the window to take in the precious moments before reading the adoption letters. She took her favorite dishes out of the cupboard, which all had different poems engraved inside the ware. After placing the food on the table, The Lady set out the plates. She then called out to each of the little girls. "Reba! Marilyn! Katherine! Victoria! Caroline! Come and eat! Time for dinner!"

Hearing their names called, they all ran inside and washed their hands in the basin before sitting down. Each of them surprisingly noticed that their names were handwritten in pink on the back of the wooden kitchen chairs. After sitting in their assigned chairs, they all took notice of the poems engraved in pink on the beautiful, white, shiny china plates as The Lady continued to bring food to the table.

As the orphans stared at the beautiful plates with engraved poems, each girl began looking at one another, sharing a sense of gratitude by the abundance of love shown towards them by their loving caretaker. The Lady in Pink then went and stood over the orphans and suggested, "How about we all take turns reading the poem on the plate? Marilyn let's start with you, okay?" Marilyn shook her head up and down with excitement. The Lady then walked over to her chair to assist her.

With the help of The Lady in Pink, Marilyn read, *"With kisses and hugs, I can snuggle like a bug."*

The Lady in Pink then moved over to Reba to help her read, but Reba insisted to The Lady that she could read by herself. After a smile and nod from The Lady, Reba glanced down at her plate and read, *"With happiness and cheers, I can chase away my fears."*

"My turn! And I need help to read," shouted Katherine. The Lady walked over by Katherine and both read aloud, *"As the moon brightens each midnight sky, so does the sun for each tear I cry."*

"I'm next! Me next!" shouted Caroline. The caretaker then went over to Caroline and they both read the poem together, *"No matter how heavy my heart may be, I can always find love underneath the Cherry Blossom Tree."*

Victoria told The Lady that her papa taught her how to read, but she would still like some help. The Lady in Pink went over to Victoria and they both read the last plate, *"Let peace be still to one and all, no matter how great, no matter how small."*

Without warning, Victoria jumped out of her chair and gave The Lady in Pink a big hug. The other girls then got out of their chairs and hugged their beloved caretaker as well.

"Oh, my sweet, little ladies! Thank you so very much!" The Lady said with a bright smile and tears in her eyes, hugging and kissing each one on top of their heads. She continued, "The message that I want you all to always keep in your hearts is that I will always cherish each of you, no matter what." She then felt a twinge of sadness and grew quiet. The Lady couldn't help but feel the menacing envelope in her apron pocket that threatened to shatter that happy moment for the precious girls. She knew that the parent adoption letters must be read to each of them; however, she decided it would be best to wait. Then, she smiled lovingly at the girls who were now looking uneasily at her. "Oh, my precious dears. From now on, everything is going to be alright," The Lady said, serving dinner. She was careful to always smile to keep the girls from fretting. It was important to the caretaker to make the orphans feel safe, happy and loved.

"After dinner, we are going to listen to some music and I will share some news with each of you."

As soon as dinner ended, The Lady walked into the living room and over to the corner to crank the phonograph. Suddenly, beautiful classical music began to play. Surprised, the girls squealed with delight. It was so soothing and relaxing that the orphans began a myriad of questions about that genre of music. The Lady gave them a brief history lesson of the music and called out names like Mozart, Beethoven, Schubert, and others.

The girls looked at each other. Marilyn whispered to Caroline, "Who did she say?"

The Lady chuckled and said, "It's okay. Most of them lived a while ago. But their music lives on and on for all of us to enjoy."

"Um, like love, right?" questioned Caroline.

"Yes. Just like love," replied The Lady with a smile.

As the music came to an end, The Lady reached inside her apron and pulled out the large envelope containing the adoption letters and sat in a chair. *This is the hardest thing I have ever had to do*, The Lady thought to herself. "Please come and sit close to me, girls."

They all huddled close to her with Victoria and Katherine sitting on her lap while the others gathered close with arms on The Lady's shoulders. "Is it a letter from my Papa? I miss him a lot," Victoria asked.

"I just want a letter from you Ms. Lady. You are my new mama now," Marilyn said.

"This is hard for me because I have grown so fond of you girls. In a few days, each of you will be joining a new family that loves children like me, but I will keep in touch with you all by writing letters, okay?" The Lady said in a sad tone.

Silence filled the room and tears began to flow from The Lady as well as the girls. "Caroline, you will join a family from New York," said The Lady wiping away her tears. Caroline embraced The Lady and buried her face in her dress. "I don't want to!" she said crying again. The Lady was finding it hard to be strong for the girls but knew this was the best for them. "Katherine, have you ever heard about Africa? You will live there with your new family. I bet you'll see many wonderful animals," said The Lady in a tender voice. "Like penguins?" asked Katherine excitedly. The Lady in Pink laughed but didn't tell her it was impossible for penguins to live in Africa." The Lady continued, "Reba, you will live with a wonderful family from

Tears of a Cherry Blossom Tree

France." Reba blurted out in excitement, "France! Oh, I love France so much! It's the greatest place in the world! Wait—Where is France?" The Lady laughed so hard that Victoria and Katherine almost fell out of her lap. The Lady in Pink composed herself and gave Reba a brief history lesson of France. "Victoria, your family will be coming from Japan. They have many beautiful Cherry Blossom Trees like ours," informed The Lady. "What's Ja-pan?" asked Victoria. The Lady told her about the fascinating culture of Japan. The Lady in Pink then looked at Marilyn, "You, my dear, will be right here in Georgia, only a few hours away. You will be adopted by a wonderful and loving lady." Marilyn softly replied, "Will she be like you? I want her to be like you." The girls began to cry as they hugged their caretaker.

After she finished reading the letters, the orphans went to their rooms and fell fast asleep. The Lady continued to sit up most of the night, unable to sleep. *What am I going to do when they're all gone? This is not easy when I care for them all so very much and have to let go,"* said The Lady to herself. When morning came, the little ones quickly ate their breakfast and rushed outside where they played, danced, and skipped around the tree. Tired from all the fun and play, the children decided to rest under the Cherry Blossom Tree and exchange tales of their dreams from the night before.

"I dreamed that I was adopted by a tall man from France," giggled Reba.

"I had a dream that I was adopted by a nice lady and man from New York," said Caroline.

"I dreamed that a nice family from Ja-pan adopted me," said Victoria.

"I had a dream that I was playing with nice penguins in Africa. Oh! And I had a nice family too," exclaimed Katherine.

"I dreamed that I was adopted by a pretty lady," said Marilyn.

After sharing their dreams, they all stood up and joined hands around the Cherry Blossom Tree. "Let's pick lots of blossoms to take with us," Reba proposed.

"Okay," Katherine agreed.

"When we miss each other, we can always look at them," Marilyn said. They envisioned living with their adopted dream families while singing a new song. *"Up and down we go, now hop and touch your toes, skip around the Cherry Blossom Tree, now stop and touch your nose."* After singing and playing, the girls went inside the orphanage to cool off.

Later that afternoon, a glossy, tuxedo-black Ford Model-T honked outside of the orphanage. The curious girls ran to the window and started oohing and aahing while giggling at the sight of the strange, shiny vehicle sitting outside. Suddenly, a wealthy looking man in a white suit and white hat with a red-striped band stepped out of the vehicle and walked toward the orphanage. On his way to the door, he spoke to the girls as they continued to peek out the window. "Bonjour, petites filles."

They all stared at each other while trying to figure out what he had said.

The man then made a goofy face at the girls and smiled, causing the girls to giggle again.

By that time, The Lady in Pink opened the door to greet the man in French. "Bonjour, Monsieur, Lambert," she politely said.

"Bonjour. Vous devez être La Dame en Rose, n'est-ce pas?"

"C'est vrai. Nous vous attendions. Bienvenue."

"Thank you," the man said with an accent.

He came inside after the greetings and formally sat on the living room couch. "Your French is very good, mademoiselle. Have you been to France before?" he asked.

"No, I have not. When I was a child, my father traveled to France and many other countries for work, where he learned to speak different languages. When he came home, he would teach my mother and I French, Japanese, German, and a few other languages," replied

The Lady. She then served the man tea as she exchanged papers for him to sign. Moments later, The Lady looked at Reba and hesitantly motioned for her to come near, dabbing her eyes with a handkerchief and feeling mixed emotions of dread and serendipity. *I've got to be strong for Reba,* The Lady thought to herself.

Upon approaching where The Lady and the French gentleman were sitting, Reba observed the man smiling at her. The Lady explained to Reba that she has been adopted and will be leaving for France.

"No! No! No! I can't leave my friends!" screamed Reba.

Without saying a word, the man smiled, then pulled a gift box out of his pocket and handed it to her.

She became silent and took the box. Then, she opened it delicately and observed a small portrait of her new family.

"They all look happy," Reba said, staring at the portrait and then up at The Lady.

The Lady wiped her eyes, smiled and then nodded, giving Reba her blessing to go with the kind gentleman. The caretaker rushed into Reba's room and came back out with Reba's suitcase, placing it on the floor by the front entrance. Before Reba left the house with the French man, she turned and hugged The Lady and the girls. The girls hugged and cried while giving Reba fresh pink Cherry Blossoms as gifts.

"It's hard letting go but she is going to be with a wonderful family," The Lady told the girls. "We all will miss her, but they have to leave soon to board their ship," the sadness was apparent in her voice.

Reba quickly gave everyone one last hug and then grabbed the polite man's hand shyly. He picked up her suitcase from the floor and walked out the door with Reba. As they drove away, Reba waved goodbye and blew kisses to The Lady and her orphan sisters.

CHAPTER THREE

NAMESAKE CARVINGS

*A*fter watching the car drive away, the girls huddled together and began crying again. They would miss Reba and couldn't bear the thought of being without her.

The Lady came into the kitchen and reassured them that everything was going to be alright. "Reba deserves a good family, and so do you all," she said, hugging them.

"I don't want to leave you," said Marilyn.

The Lady smiled and looked at each girl, "Life takes us all on different journeys and far away from the people we care about sometimes, but life also has a way of bringing us all back together."

For the rest of the day, the orphans distracted themselves from the nagging thoughts of missing Reba by playing games. As they were playing games, the little girls all decided to carve Reba's name in the Cherry Blossom Tree which read, *Reba, we love and miss you.*

When sunset approached, The Lady in Pink called the girls inside for dinner. After everyone finished their meals, The Lady and her beloved orphans swapped bittersweet stories of Reba, talks of her love of singing and dancing were the main subjects of their conversation. During the conversations, the girls started yawning from their long emotional day; The Lady in Pink saw the exhaustion in their little faces and told them to take their baths, promising she would read stories to them afterwards. After bathing, the children eagerly piled into the Lady in Pink's bed, and as soon as The Lady's soothing voice started to tell a story, the orphans fell asleep one by one. The Lady looked down at them and smiled, deciding to let the precious girls remain in the bed with her for the night.

The next morning, there was a knock at the door that had awakened everyone in the orphanage. The Lady hurried to the door and peeked outside, seeing a Japanese lady with two young Japanese girls. She opened the door and greeted them, "Ohayou Gozaimasu."

"Ohayou," greeted the Japanese lady. "Watashi wa Izumi Sachiko desu. Yoroshiku Onegaishimasu," she continued.

"Nice to meet you too, Mrs. Izumi, and who are these little angels with you?" asked The Lady in Pink.

"These are my two daughters, Mihoko and Akane," Mrs. Izumi said with an accent. "My husband, Miyato, is away on business and here are the signed adoption papers. We are here to pick up Victoria Simmons," uttered Mrs. Izumi, politely bowing.

"Naruhodo…Watashitachi wa anata wo matteita," said The Lady.

"You were waiting for me? That is good. I am impressed with your Japanese. Where did you learn to speak it?" asked Mrs. Izumi.

"My father taught me Japanese and other languages as a small child," said The Lady. She then softly smiled and sighed, "He passed away when I was quite young. Now, I suppose I study and practice speaking different languages as a way to keep him alive."

When Victoria overheard the conversation, she screamed, "Please don't let them take me away, I don't want to leave!" The other girls held her tightly and told her not to worry.

The Lady in Pink apologized and invited Mrs. Izumi and her daughters inside for breakfast. She then called for the girls to come into the kitchen area to greet the guests. Victoria followed the other girls hesitantly with her arms covering her face. Tears flowed like a stream and sniffling sounds were heard amongst the girls, who were attempting to guide Victoria, blinded with tears, to her favorite chair. Curiously eyeing Mrs. Izumi and her daughters through her hidden, tear-stained face, Victoria sat down quietly.

Mrs. Izumi wasted no time introducing herself and her family. As breakfast was served, Mrs. Izumi gave Victoria a bag that had a gift in it. Victoria's little arms quickly came down from her face and snatched the bag with excitement. Reaching into the bag, Victoria pulled out a gift-wrapped box and opened it. Inside, she found a porcelain, Cherry Blossom doll that was labeled, *A gift from Kurobe-shi, Japan.*

Mrs. Izumi knew that Victoria's father was killed in war from the adoption agency's report received. Knowing this, she told Victoria that the Izumi family would care for her as her father would have wished. After breakfast, Victoria grabbed her suitcase from The Lady in Pink. Tears flowed from the eyes of The Lady and the girls as they hugged Victoria for the last time. As Mrs. Izumi, her daughters, and Victoria exited the orphanage, Mrs. Izumi bowed and said to everyone, "Sayonara."

"Sayonara," replied The Lady with a bow and a wave. The orphans walked out onto the front porch singing their rhyme, "*Up and down we go...*" while waving goodbye to their dear friend. When the Izumi family and Victoria loaded onto a carriage that was waiting for them outside, the orphans ran off the porch and started chasing it as went down the road, waving at Victoria. The newly adopted orphan looked back as she traveled down the road and waved back to her Stillwaters friends, whom she reckoned she would never see again.

The next day, the girls decided to spend some time outside and look at the flower garden in the backyard. Suddenly, the orphans heard someone whistling the song, *"Yankee Doodle."*

Then, they heard knocking at the front door. The children rushed inside the house through the backdoor to see who was at the front of the orphanage. Once the girls were inside, they saw a lady and a man dressed in high fashion standing outside the open front door talking with The Lady in Pink. Soon after, The Lady in Pink and the fashionable couple walked inside and headed to the living room. The girls curiously followed their guardian and the couple, meanwhile, the little girls pondered who the well-dressed couple would adopt next. The Lady in Pink exchanged adoption papers with the New York couple and then looked at Caroline. "Come here, darling. I want you to meet your new family," said The Lady with tears welling up in her eyes.

"I'm Betty and this is Jim, my husband," spoke the woman. "We are delighted to have you join our family. Here's a doll for you."

"Thank you," Caroline mumbled to the couple while staring at the doll.

"Give me a hug, sweetie, I'm going to miss you so much, don't you ever forget," The Lady said. Each of the girls handed Caroline a pink blossom and hugged her.

"We will take good care of you," said Betty as she took Caroline by the hand.

"Here, let me help you with your suitcase," said Jim. Off they went, waving as they exited the orphanage.

Marilyn and Katherine both stood alongside The Lady in Pink and waved goodbye with tears of joy, but even more sadness. "Come on girls, let's go inside and get some goodies," The Lady said. As they entered the orphanage, The Lady reached into the kitchen cupboard for sticks of peppermint candies.

"Can I have one?" shouted Katherine with excitement.

"What about me? I want one too?" Marilyn said in a whining voice.

"I have one for each of you," The Lady said as she gave each of them a piece of candy. "I guess it will be okay if I join you all," The Lady said.

"Yes, thank you for the candy. It is really good and tasty," Marilyn said in a sweet voice. "Thank you, I like this candy," Katherine uttered.

Later in the day, they all gathered in the living room area to listen to music and play games. "I will leave you two girls to enjoy the music and games while I make dinner for us," The Lady said. She then announced the menu, "We are having fried chicken, cornbread, green beans, mash potatoes with gravy and freshly brewed tea."

Both Marilyn and Katherine began jumping up and down with excitement. "I love chicken and sweet tea," Katherine said in a thrilled tone.

"I like to eat everything," Marilyn said in a soft voice.

They both began dancing, singing and playing more games in the living room until dinner was ready. The Lady in Pink overheard their conversations. *They are so funny,* said The Lady to herself while giggling and preparing dinner.

"Ouch! That hurts! You stepped on my foot—on purpose!" suddenly shouted Marilyn, breaking the serene moment.

"I don't care. You shouldn't have bumped against me," Katherine said. In a fit of anger, Marilyn shoved Katherine into the phonograph, causing the music to skip. Katherine then retaliated by kicking Marilyn in the shin. Marilyn was so infuriated that she pulled Katherine by the hair and shoved her against the wall.

The Lady in Pink heard the loud commotions coming from the living room as she was cooking dinner. "Girls, are you all still having fun?" The Lady in Pink asked, curious of the noise.

"Um—Yes, we are having a great time. I love this music," Marilyn replied in a sweet tone, not wanting to alarm The Lady of the fighting.

"I am dancing with Marilyn," Katherine fibbed while licking out her tongue at Marilyn.

"Great, dinner will be ready shortly and I will call you when it is ready," The Lady in Pink said.

"Okay, it smells so good, can't wait!" shouted Katherine, pulling Marilyn's hair.

"I have not had one problem since these girls arrived. Thank the Lord. I couldn't have been blessed with any better girls to care for," The Lady in Pink said to herself as she looked up to heaven.

Moments later, the bumping noises grew louder, and then a sound of glass breaking came from the living room. "Are you two alright?" The Lady in Pink asked, being suspicious of the two girls.

"Yes, I accidentally tripped over the table and a vase fell and broke while we were dancing. I'm alright," Marilyn said.

"It's time for dinner, you both can come to the table. I will clean up the mess later," The Lady in Pink said.

Suddenly, Marilyn and Katherine stopped in the middle of the fight, holding each other's hair. "I won," Katherine whispered while glaring at Marilyn with a smirk.

"No, I won," Marilyn said, staring back at Katherine with a missing tooth. They both let go of each other's hair and walked slowly into the kitchen area. Marilyn was conscious to keep her mouth closed to hide her missing tooth from The Lady. Their dresses were ravaged and ripped, and both orphan's faces were red, with small scratches and wild and tangled hair. They sat down as The Lady in Pink was preparing dishes with her back turned to them.

"Ah!" The Lady in Pink shrieked after she turned around and seen the girls' faces. "This can't be true. Is this a nightmare or have you two been fighting?" she asked, frowning at the two orphans.

"No, we were dancing and having fun," Katherine replied.

"That's not true. She stepped on my foot and we started fighting," Marilyn mumbled.

"I can't believe what I'm seeing. They both look like they have been in a chicken fight," The Lady in Pink thought to herself while shaking her head. "We will talk about this after dinner," The Lady said in disappointment.

"Yummy! That smells good," Marilyn uttered.

"I want a big piece of chicken," Katherine said. The Lady in Pink served dinner and sat with the girls.

"I will say the blessing—Marilyn! What happened to your tooth?!" The Lady yelled.

"Oh, I don't know, it was already kind of wobbly. But now I can see the tooth fairy, right?" giggled Marilyn.

"What's a blessing?" Katherine interrupted.

"Quiet, Katherine, you are in enough trouble," The Lady scolded.

"What about Marilyn? She hit me too."

"Both of you. No talking," The Lady said in a stern tone while putting her finger to her lips. "Lord, thank you for the food and we ask your blessings upon each of us. Help us to treat each other with respect and love. Amen," prayed The Lady.

"Who is the Lord?" Marilyn asked.

"He is someone that wants us all to be kind to one another," answered The Lady.

"I have never seen him before. When is he coming over?" Katherine asked, staring at the front door.

Dinner was served with the girls eating, smacking, and drinking their tea. Later during dinner, there was a knock at the door.

"That must be the Lord!" shouted Katherine.

The Lady in Pink opened the door and recognized the old, gawky farmer and his wife. "Yes, how are you all doing?" The Lady politely asked.

"Well, we could explain better if you would let us in!" snidely replied the farmer.

The Lady allowed both the farmer and his wife to enter. "These are our distant neighbors, Cleotus and Rosey. They just stopped by for a moment," The Lady said.

Both Cleotus and Rosey stared at the girls in an intense state of shock and horror. "We smelled the chicken and wanted to see if you were okay. We saw some carriages leaving here with kids the other day," Rosey said.

"Good Lawd, what happen to these young'un's? They look like they been fightin' with my chickens. Hair all stickin up, a missing tooth, scratches, red swollen faces. How y'all doing?" Cleotus asked.

"You look funny," said Katherine giggling.

"What's so funny young un?" Cleotus asked.

"You are cross-eyed with missing teeth like Marilyn," Katherine joked. The children both began laughing at Cleotus as he glared at them, not cracking a smile.

"Well, I better be gettin down this here road. These young'uns are rotten," said Cleotus.

"Just like your teeth," Katherine said laughing.

"He is smelly too with no hair on top of his head!" Marilyn said laughing.

The Lady in Pink prepared both Cleotus and Rosey a plate before they left. "Girls! Be respectful," The Lady in Pink said, feeling slightly embarrassed after the orphans' comments.

"Yes ma'am," Katherine said.

As Cleotus turned to leave, there was a huge gaping hole in the back of his pants, The Lady and the girls all laughed at the scene.

Rosey turned to see what everyone was laughing about and noticed the hole in Cleotus's pants; she then shook her head in embarrassment for her husband and laughed along with The Lady and the girls.

Not thinking, Cleotus grabbed a hot, sizzling chicken leg from the cast iron skillet. He immediately started blowing his hands and yelling in pain as he scurried out the front door. "Ouch! Good Lawd, this here chicken is too hot."

They all followed Cleotus outside, pointing at the funniest scene of him running down the dirt road and losing a shoe.

"Thank you all and it looks like I better be going. Cleotus is going to need some ice, a shoe, and definitely some patches to cover up those holes in his church trousers. He is always a mess," said Rosey, laughing and waving goodbye.

The Lady in Pink and the girls laughed at Cleotus while waving back to Rosey. Soon after, they returned inside the orphanage to finish their dinner.

"Now, girls, that still doesn't excuse you two from your bad behavior. I hope the living room is not a mess when I check it later. Go ahead and finish your dinner," The Lady said.

The girls' eyes widened as they stared at each other with guilt on their faces while finishing their meal in silence. As dinner came to an end, The Lady got up to make her way into the living room.

Before she entered, Katherine suddenly fell out of her chair with cornbread in her hand. Within seconds, Marilyn does the same thing with a chicken wing in her hand. The Lady rushed over to Katherine and then to Marilyn. Unable to wake either of them, she decided to dip a washcloth in cold water to pat their faces. After failing to get a response, she checked their breathing and noticed everything seemed normal. She decided to pick Katherine up and carry her to bed. On the way, she peeked into the living room and gasped at the mess the two orphans made. "Oh my, this is unbelievable. It's worse than I imagined!" exclaimed The Lady in Pink aloud. She then looked down at Katherine, noticing one of her eyes slightly peeking. "Katherine, can you hear me?" The Lady asked. Quickly, Katherine's eye closed.

The Lady decided to take both she and Marilyn to her bedroom for the night. After The Lady tucked them in, she headed out of the bedroom and left the bedroom door slightly ajar. The caretaker curiously peeked back through the ajar door and witnessed the sneaky girls peeking at each other with one eye closed. "*I knew this was too strange to be true,*" said The Lady to herself. The Lady then proceeded to clean up the living room before morning. She reached inside her apron and read Marilyn's adoption letter. The Lady noticed that she was to leave the next day and tears streamed down her cheeks. Instead of scolding the girls, she prepared letters of love for both Katherine and Marilyn with a stick of peppermint candy on top of each. The Lady found Marilyn's tooth lying on the Livingroom floor and kept it to put under Marilyn's pillow. She later retired for the night after cleaning up the mess and climbed into bed alongside the girls for the night. Later, Marilyn nudged The Lady with her elbow.

"Are you alright dear?" The Lady asked Marilyn.

"No, I just want to say I'm sorry for fighting. Do you forgive me?" Marilyn asked.

"Of course, I forgive you, my sweet Marilyn, and I accept your apology. I am so glad you two did not go to bed angry. Every day is a gift and we should always treasure it. It's more important that we never take the gift of love for each other for granted. Tomorrow is not promised to anyone," The Lady explained. Just as they all were going off to sleep, Katherine nudged The Lady with her elbow.

"Katherine, are you okay?"

"I'm sorry too, for lying and fighting. I knocked Marilyn's tooth out by accident," Katherine apologized.

"I forgive you, and I'm proud of you too dear," The Lady smiled and kissed them both on their foreheads. Marilyn and Katherine then reached across The Lady to hug each other.

"Good night, girls," The Lady said.

"Good night," replied Marilyn.

"Good night," Katherine slurred as she was fading into sleep.

All cuddled together in one bed, they peacefully went off to sleep. Soon as the morning sunshine peeked through the bedroom window, they all got up and hugged each other.

"Marilyn, someone left something underneath your pillow," The Lady said.

"What could it be?" Marilyn questioned while slowly digging under her pillow.

"Wow! It's a penny!" she shouted with excitement.

"The good tooth fairy left it for you after finding your tooth on the living room floor," The Lady said.

"But, I wasn't good," Marilyn said.

"The good fairy forgives you as well," The Lady explained.

"She must be nice," Marilyn thought out loud.

"Hmm, why, yes. She is quite nice I suppose," The Lady chuckled and continued, "Okay girls, let's get up and take our baths. After you both are clean, I will make biscuits, bacon and eggs. How does that sound?" The girls smiled, nodding up and down.

After bathing and changing into fresh clothing, The Lady escorted them both into the living room area. "The mess is gone and someone left letters with candy," Marilyn stated, puzzled.

The Lady then looked down adoringly at both girls and said, "The letters and candies are for you both. You may have them later." She then led them to the kitchen. "You two can help make breakfast," The Lady said.

"Yes, Ma'am," Katherine replied.

"Thank you for the letter and candy, I love you, Lady in Pink," Marilyn said.

"I love you too, Ms. Lady in Pink," Katherine said.

"The Lady's eyes started to water from the girls' loving words. The caretaker cleared her throat as she responded, "You're welcome, and I love you both, dearly." The Lady paused for a few seconds and stared lovingly at Marilyn and Katherine, appreciating her last moments with them. She started to reflect on all of the girls that came to the orphanage and then felt a sadness. The Lady didn't want to ruin the moment with sadness, so she perked up and said to the girls, "Now, it's time to join in making breakfast. Let me get you both an apron," The Lady said. She reached for two aprons and had both girls to stand up in their chairs as she put the aprons on them. "I will cook the bacon and eggs, and you girls can help me with the biscuits.

After preparing breakfast, they all gathered to eat. "Don't forget the blessing," reminded Katherine.

"Why don't you say it for us this time?" The Lady suggested.

"Um, okay—Thank you Lord for blessing the food and… for not letting us get a spanking last night. The end," prayed Katherine.

The Lady turned her head, struggling not to laugh at Katherine's prayer. The Lady cleared her throat and composed herself, "That was a wonderful prayer, Katherine. Now let's eat."

Just as they were about to finish breakfast, there was a knock at the door.

"Finish your breakfast girls, I'll return shortly," The Lady said as she left the breakfast table.

In the doorway stood a lady with papers. "Good Morning, my name is Maria and I have adoption papers for Marilyn Clisby," she said.

"Please come in, Maria. I have been expecting you," The Lady said.

Maria entered the orphanage holding a white poodle. The girls both jumped out of their seats with excitement.

"Oh wow! It's a puppy. She's pretty and nice," Marilyn said. "Can I hold her?" she asked, excitedly holding her arms out.

"Sure, but it's actually a boy, not a girl," Maria replied as she carefully placed the poodle in Marilyn's arms.

"Oh, his hair is soft like cotton," Marilyn said as she held the puppy and rubbed her cheek on the poodle's head.

"Yes, it is. His name is Shakespeare," Maria replied with a big grin.

"He is so sweet," Katherine exclaimed as she petted the puppy.

"Marilyn, my name is Maria and I will be taking care of you from now on," she said.

"Where do you live?" Marilyn asked.

"I live in the North Georgia Mountains, where the air is so fresh. You will enjoy the scenery," Maria replied.

"Well, I have to pack my clothes," Marilyn sadly stated. She slowly got down from the kitchen table, handed the poodle over to Katherine, and started walking to her room with The Lady in Pink following behind her.

"I will be back shortly. I must help her pack. Katherine, will you keep Ms. Maria and Shakespeare company for me?" The Lady asked.

"Um, hum," Katherine replied.

As The Lady helped Marilyn to pack, tears ran down both of their cheeks. "I will always love you and write to you," cried Marilyn.

"I will always love you as well, and I promise to write back to every letter you send," The Lady told her, wiping away tears.

After packing, they hugged each other tightly. They then went back to the kitchen and saw Katherine playing with the puppy. "I have to go, Katherine. Um, maybe I will see you again one day," Marilyn said.

"Yeah, maybe. I don't want you to leave," Katherine replied in somber tone with her head down. Seconds later, they both ran and embraced each other one last time. The Lady signed the papers and they all exited onto the front porch of the orphanage. Maria carried the suitcase and Marilyn kissed The Lady and Katherine goodbye as she held her puppy.

"Goodbye," Maria said.

"Bye!" Marilyn said.

"Goodbye," The Lady said.

Katherine cried, "What about me? Why not me? Can I go too?"

The Lady in Pink embraced her, then lifted Katherine's chin and stared lovingly into her eyes. "There is a family who is out there waiting for a special little girl like you. You'll see," said The Lady tenderly. She then hugged Katherine with watery eyes. The Lady in Pink had come to the point of sadness after realizing she was down to one child.

As Marilyn and Maria began walking towards a carriage in the distance, Marilyn, still walking towards the carriage, looked back at Katherine and loudly sang, *"Up and down we go, our tears will be no more, skip around the Cherry Blossom Tree, now love's come to our door."* Katherine was teary-eyed as she mumbled the lyrics with her friend, who she may never see again.

As the carriage took off down the road, The Lady looked down and placed her hand on Katherine's little shoulder.

The Lady reached inside the pocket of her apron and took out five pink ribbons to represent each child. She showed Katherine how to tie them around the Cherry Blossom Tree.

"Why are you doing that?" she asked.

"They represent all five of you girls," replied The Lady, trying not to cry.

After they tied the ribbons, Katherine helped The Lady carved the rest of the names of the adopted girls into the tree. *"Caroline, Reba, Victoria and Marilyn. All of the names are here except one,"* said The Lady to herself. The Lady in Pink struggled inside knowing that she would soon have to carve Katherine's name in the tree alone. After having the pleasure of loving the orphans, The Lady found her heart breaking with deep sadness. She thought to herself, *"My heart doesn't have the strength to go through this again, but I must be strong. I must be strong for Katherine. Maybe I can adopt her! No, I couldn't even if I wanted to. The arrangements are already final through the agency. Hopefully, this last family never shows up. Oh no, how selfish of me. God, please give me the strength to let go of this last precious child."*

"Katherine, will you sit under the tree with me?"

"Um, hum, I like playing with blossoms. Here, let me sprinkle some on your head," Katherine said as she lovingly sprinkled pink blossoms in The Lady's honey-brown hair.

"Tell me about your granny, Katherine."

"My granny was nice and always made my favorite treats. You are nice, like her."

"Thank you, and I bet you are just as sweet and nice as your granny was," The Lady said.

"Are you going to get some more girls like me?"

"You all are my first and last group of wonderful girls here at Stillwaters' Orphanage. But, I hope that you girls will one day carry on my journey of taking care of beautiful orphaned children, wherever you are in the world or even right here at Stillwaters, after I'm gone," The Lady said.

"I will carry on your journey Ms. Lady in Pink, and I promise to teach them how to make delicious Cherry Blossom muffins too."

The Lady let out a laugh and said, "Let's go inside and prepare dinner."

After dinner, The Lady read bedtime stories to Katherine, and they both fell fast asleep.

CHAPTER FOUR

HOMEWARD BOUND FOR AFRICA

The next morning, they both were awaken by the warmth of the sunshine gleaming through the bedroom window. The Lady yawned and stretched, then she looked over at Katherine and said with a smile, "Good morning little lady. It seems like it's going to be a beautiful day, doesn't it?"

"Umm humm. And I'm hungry and ready for breakfast," responded Katherine, gleefully. They leaped out of bed, brushed their teeth, washed their faces and headed to the kitchen. The Lady allowed Katherine to beat the eggs while she made biscuits. The smell of bacon filled the air as it crackled on the stove. While the food was still cooking, Katherine pleaded and begged The Lady for something to eat. As the bacon came off the stove top, Katherine quickly placed her plate out on the table. The Lady chuckled and made sure Katherine had more than enough. After breakfast, they washed dishes together, and when everything was cleaned and put away, they both went out and sat underneath the Cherry Blossom Tree.

A feeling of depression and loneliness came crashing down on them, obliterating the warm, happy feeling they had earlier that morning. Wordlessly, they both started to reminisce about the days gone by. It was all about enjoying their last moments together. The Lady in Pink wanted to liven things up a bit, so she loudly started singing, *"Up and down we go, now hop and touch your toes, skip around the Cherry Blossom Tree, now stop and touch your nose."* They played games around the tree for a few minutes and then skipped into the house. The most beautiful white dove cooed as it flew over the house. The Lady in Pink looked up at the dove and smiled.

Moments later, The Lady in Pink entered the kitchen and mixed ingredients to make her favorite Cherry Blossom muffins.

"I want to help," pleaded Katherine

"Of course," responded The Lady.

She gave Katherine a spoon, and they began mixing the ingredients.

After the ingredients were mixed and placed in the oven, Katherine licked the spoon, bowl, and her fingers. The Lady smiled, seeing the muffin dough all over Katherine's face, hands, and hair. As soon as Katherine finished licking the dough, The Lady washed her up and read her a book in the living room. Katherine sat on The Lady in Pink's lap as she listened to the story.

In the middle of the caretaker reading a story, Katherine unexpectedly leaped down as the aroma of muffins filled the air and began dancing. When The Lady asked her about the name of the dance, Katherine told her, "It is called *The Cherry Blossom Shuffle.*" She began shuffling and tapping her feet while gliding across the kitchen floor. The Lady chuckled so hard that she started crying. After becoming exhausted from dancing and laughter, Katherine flopped down on the couch breathing heavily.

The Lady applauded enthusiastically. "I truly enjoyed the performance. Oh! The muffins are ready now, it is time to put on the icing," she said, still laughing at Katherine's performance. After the delicious treat cooled, The Lady spread pink icing on top of the muffins.

"Wow! It looks yummy!" Katherine exclaimed. "Can I have one, two or… three?" she asked.

"Yes, you may have three, if you like," laughed The Lady.

The Lady placed the muffins on a plate and Katherine yelled, "Thank you!"

The Lady in Pink laughed heartily. *I will desperately miss my sweet Katherine,* she thought to herself, feeling an overwhelming rush of sadness.

Out of nowhere, sounds of many loud drums were heard coming towards the orphanage. Katherine ran to the window and witnessed, in awe, the most beautiful parade of people approaching the orphanage. "Look! Look! Come look at the beautiful robes and hats they are wearing! I love their beautiful clothes!" shouted Katherine.

As the marching drummers in robes made their way to the orphanage's porch steps, the loud drums made one final *Ka-boom!* and suddenly stopped altogether. Knocks were heard coming from the front door. The sound of the knocks caused The Lady's heart to sink into deep despair. Standing in the kitchen, The Lady almost lost her balance. Then, she steadied herself by placing her hands on the kitchen's table. Her head was down with teary closed eyes; she found herself momentarily paralyzed by the threatening knocks at the door. *"Stay strong. Stay strong for Katherine,"* The Lady kept repeating to herself.

Seconds later, Katherine came running into the kitchen, questioning, "Don't you hear the knocks at the door?"

Tears of a Cherry Blossom Tree

The Lady quickly wiped her eyes, smiled, and nodded to Katherine. Katherine looked up at her loving caretaker and smiled; the last orphan gently grabbed the Lady's hand and they both walked slowly towards the door together. The Lady finally opened the door and said, "Welcome to Stillwaters' Orphanage! You must be Ma'am Kizi and I'm so terribly sorry about the wait!"

Ma'am Kizi, her family and staff from Africa replied in unison, smiling, "Asanti!" meaning thank you.

"Your skin is so beautiful and I love your hair," Katherine remarked to the new guest.

Ma'am Kizi then responded to Katherine, "Why, thank you, darling. Oh my, I love your rose-golden hair and those gorgeous blue eyes. Your skin is just as beautiful."

"Oh, dear, where are my manners today? I'm so sorry again, Ma'am Kizi, please, please, come inside. Your family are all welcomed as well. How many people came with you, fifteen, maybe? I can make some tea for you all," insisted The Lady.

"That's quite alright, dear, and no need for apologies. We will graciously decline the tea, I don't want you to go through the trouble. It's such a beautiful day outside and we are fine right here. Besides, my family, and especially my bodyguards, can be a bit clumsy at times, so it's best that they stay out here," Ma'am Kizi snickered, winking at The Lady and Katherine.

Then, Ma'am Kizi smiled and gave Katherine a sapphire robe with a head covering symbolizing Ma'am Kizi's family of royalty and wealth. She eagerly took the clothes and ran to her room to change into them.

In the meantime, The Lady in Pink signed off on the adoption papers to release Katherine to the African family. "I know that Katherine will be in good hands after reading the report about your beautiful family and their royalty. I also know that she will be well-rounded as you prepare her for the future," The Lady said.

"With the help of God, I hope to teach her to become a great doctor one day. It's very rare for women to be doctors, and seemingly impossible to be an African, woman doctor, but royalty has its privileges," replied Ma'am Kizi with a grin and another wink.

"I love it! It's so beautiful! Look at me!" Katherine shouted as she came running back to The Lady and Ma'am Kizi. She grinned and modeled her African wardrobe. They all clapped, cheered, and danced to the sounds of the drums. After seeing the exchange of the adoption papers, Katherine smiled solemnly. "I am finally adopted by a family. Can I write you letters from Africa every day? I will tell you all about the penguins."

"Yes, you certainly may," said The Lady with a smile, still wiping away tears.

Katherine grabbed her tightly by the neck and whispered, "I love you with all of my heart, and you will always be my new mama. When I get older, I will take care of little girls, right here, just like you."

The Lady burst into tears again and cried, "I know you will, and I love you too, my sweet Katherine." She then handed Katherine her suitcase and kissed her on the cheek while whispering, *"As the moon brightens each midnight sky, so does the sun for each tear I cry."*

The drums started up again, and Katherine danced out the door, joining the parade as they stroll down the road.

"Kwa heri!" they screamed while heading off into the sunset towards a line of carriages parked down the road.

After Katherine left, The Lady in Pink, wearing a long, pink flowery dress, walked outside underneath the Cherry Blossom Tree and carved Katherine's name into it. She then closed her teary-eyes and sung, *"Up and down I go. How I will miss them—so."* The caretaker began to sob as she thought of her new reality without her precious orphans.

As she thought back of her time with the children, a white dove came down from the sky and hovered in front of The Lady. *"I believe I know what you are dove. If you are, what I think you are, take care of my girls,"* The Lady said to herself as though she was speaking to the dove. The dove seemed to be trying to convey a message to The Lady before it returned to the sky, but the message was a mystery to the caretaker. Almost a month after the orphans left with their new families, The Lady in Pink decided to explore the world and write the girls letters about her travels. On special occasions and celebrations, she would accept invitations to attend events supporting them throughout adulthood.

Reba's Adoption Journey

"I am so glad to have you join us in France. Also, I think you will enjoy the schools, parks and foods there," said the Frenchman.

"I love food and treats. You do have treats, don't you?" Reba asked.

"Sure, here's a peppermint stick that I brought you."

"Thank you. I love candy. The Lady in Pink gave us candy and muffins all the time."

"How sweet of her. You will have lots of treats waiting for you when we arrive in France."

"What kind of treats?"

"Chocolate, licorice, peppermint, and taffy," answered the Frenchman.

After a few hours of traveling from Stillwaters' Orphanage, Reba and the Frenchmen finally arrived at the seaport, where people were boarding ships and cargo was being loaded and unloaded.

"Well, it looks like we made it to the right place," the Frenchman said to Reba with a grin.

"Look at those big ships, I want to get on. Are you scared?" Reba asked as she peered curiously.

"No, I love riding on ships and seeing the beautiful ocean. I will park here at the dock and take our suitcases on board."

Once on board, the Frenchman took Reba on to the top deck as the ship sailed. "Look, those birds are following us," said Reba

"Those are seagulls and they love to eat food that passengers throw overboard. Here, let me show you." The Frenchman took a piece of bread and threw it overboard. A seagull swooped down and ate it as it landed in the ocean.

"Wow! Did you see that?"

The Frenchman chuckled at Reba's reaction. "I did, and now it's your turn. Take this piece of bread and throw it overboard."

"Look! Look! He's going to get it. Yes! He got it. Did you see that?" Reba asked

"Yes, and did you enjoy that?"

"Yes, it was fun," Reba replied smiling. "What's your name, again?"

"My name is Nathan and I am glad that you are coming home with us. You are going to enjoy meeting your new family."

"Are they nice?"

"Of course, and they will treat you very good," said Nathan.

"You're nicer than my stepfather. He was mean to me."

"I will always be nice to you and treat you as my daughter."

Many weeks later, the ship docked in France. Nathan and Reba unloaded before heading to her new home. Upon arrival, Nathan's wife and son hurried outside to greet Reba as they exited the vehicle. They helped take her suitcase inside and presented Reba with a welcome basket of goodies. "Wow! Is that for me?" asked Reba.

"It is for you and Welcome Home, Reba. I'm Camila and it's so good to finally meet you. Oh, and this is our wonderful son Ethan," said Nathan's wife, while smiling.

"This is a big house. It looks like a doll house. Do you have dolls in here?" Reba asked.

"No, but we do have lots of fun here. Please feel free to walk around and get to know your new home, and Ethan, please take Reba's suitcase to her room. I will be in the kitchen preparing dinner," replied Camila.

As Ethan carried Reba's suitcase upstairs, Reba roamed inside of the spacious, two-story house that had a stone exterior and reddish roof. She quickly fell in love with the many plants decorated within the five-bedroom home, some plants were on the floor and some were hanging from the tall ceilings. Moments later, Ethan ran back downstairs to talk to Reba, who was now in the dining room staring at the colorful, abstract paintings on the wall.

"Hey, I am glad you're here. I have always wanted a brother or a sister," said Ethan excitedly, brushing back his shiny black hair back with his hand.

"How old are you?" inquired Reba.

"I'm ten, but I'll be eleven in a few months. Do you like playing games and ice skating?"

"I like games, but what is ice skating?" Reba asked.

Camilla walked into the dining room from the kitchen and chimed in, "Listen, before we talk about playing games or ice skating, let's show Reba her new room upstairs. We'll eat dinner and go ice skating later."

After getting settled in, everyone enjoyed dinner, played games, and went to the local ice-skating rink, where the adoptive family began teaching Reba how to ice skate. No one ever discussed

Reba's family history for the sake of helping her move forward. Throughout the next few years, Reba enjoyed attending school, making friends, and traveling abroad with her new family. She and The Lady in Pink continued to write letters, sharing life experiences.

As she entered her teens, Reba joined her high school figure skating team, winning several singles competitions. After graduation, she received a full scholarship to college and won a silver medal in the singles 1920 European Figure Skating Championships. Reba continued to excel and eventually earned her way to competing in the singles 1922 World Figure Skating Championships, where she won three gold medals. The event was attended by her adoptive family. She also invited The Lady in Pink, Marilyn, Katherine, Caroline and Victoria to join her. It was a great reunion and celebration for everyone.

A year later, Reba left the figure skating competitions and became a celebrity spokesman for aiding abused children. She went on to become an actress in many movies and used her own story as an inspiration of hope for suffering children around the world. She later married an entrepreneur by the name of Alexandre who specialized in providing prosthetics for the disabled and remained in France.

Reba, now in her early thirties, received a troubling letter from The Lady in Pink that caused her to immediately travel back to Stillwaters.

Tears of a Cherry Blossom Tree

Victoria's Adoption Journey

Joyous memories from Stillwaters continuously replayed in Victoria's mind as she and her new adoptive family traveled down the dirt road, heading towards port.

Upon arrival at the port, Mrs. Izumi carried everyone's luggage on board the ship with Victoria, Mihoko and Akane trailing behind her, holding each other's hand. Once on board, they all entered their room and saw beautiful Japanese origamis hanging in the ceiling and porcelain dolls on the beds. Victoria curiously looked around the decorated room, then she turned and looked at Mrs. Izumi and her two girls. Unexpectantly, Victoria screamed out, "I want to go back, Now! I want my bed, and The Lady, and my friends. Take me back to them, Now!" Right after, Victoria ran into the corner of the room, curled up with her face down in her lap, and started bawling. Mrs. Izumi speedily walked over and sat on the floor next Victoria, gently rubbing her back to console her. The two children of Mrs. Izumi watched in confusion, slightly fearing the orphan after the outburst.

"Oh, Victoria, I'm sorry. I know this is all new and different, but I promise that we will love you and take great care of you, just like your family did at Stillwaters. One of the reasons I chose you was because my father died as your father did and I hoped that I could give you the love you need."

Victoria slowly raised her head with tears in her eyes and asked, "How did your papa die?"

"Well, he died trying to protect our village from some very bad people, just like your father died trying to protect America. I was just a girl when he was killed by those bad people and didn't understand why he put himself in such danger, but now I realize that men like my father and your papa sacrificed their lives for the freedom of others; It's the most heroic thing a person can do."

"I miss him a lot," Victoria wept.

"I know, sweetie, I miss my father too," replied Mrs. Izumi, wiping away a tear from her eye.

Victoria placed her head on Mrs. Izumi's lap and fell asleep within seconds. Mrs. Izumi softly rubbed Victoria's back as she slept, and then quietly whispered to her daughters to rest up for dinner.

After they slept for a few hours, Mrs. Izumi woke up and said to the girls, "Get up, girls, it's time for dinner. Hai, okinasai. Tabeyou yo." Mrs. Izumi spoke in English for Victoria and in Japanese for her daughters.

"Victoria, I have a beautiful dress just for you. It's called a kimono and many women wear them in Japan. Would you like to try it on after dinner?" Mrs. Izumi asked.

"Um, yes, and thank you," she replied, still feeling a bit hazy from sleep.

"I will teach you how to say thank you in Japanese. Now repeat after me, Arigato gozaimasu."

"A-ri-ga-to-go-zai-masu," repeated Victoria.

"Good job, I have taught many children your age the Japanese language. I am a language teacher in Japan and I will teach you more words later."

As they all entered the dining area, there was a buffet of all kinds of Japanese cuisines. "What are these?" Victoria asked pointing at the sushi buffet items.

"That's Ahi – raw tuna, Amaebi – raw sweet shrimp, Ebi – cooked tiger shrimp, Kani – cooked crab meat and Umi Masu - raw Ocean Trout and Teba – Chicken wings," answered Mrs. Izumi.

"I only want the chicken wings, and can I try a sweet shrimp?"

"Sure. Here are your chicken wings and Amaebi."

"Thank you," Victoria said. Mihoko and Akane both smiled as everyone sat down to dine. "I like the sushi and chicken," Victoria said, and Mrs. Izumi smiled. She then told Mrs. Izumi, "I want to be a teacher. Can you show me how to be a teacher like you?"

"Why, Yes!" said Mrs. Izumi smiling.

The following days of the journey allowed everyone to become acquainted with each other. They laughed and showed Victoria how to make different origamis such as butterflies and cranes.

Several weeks later, the ship docked at Japan's port. They all were excited to arrive in Japan and leave the ship for home. "Look at those buildings. I like them," Victoria said in awe, referring to the Japanese architecture.

"I am glad you like them," responded Mrs. Izumi as they were traveling home by carriage. Arriving home, everyone was greeted by Mr. Izumi who spoke very little English.

"Okaeri! Minna ga buji ni kaette kite yokatta na," said Mr. Izumi.

Mrs. Izumi translated to Victoria, "Welcome! I am glad you all arrived safely back home."

They entered the house and showed Victoria her room. "Where are the chairs?"

"In Japan, we like to sit on the floor to talk and eat," replied Mrs. Izumi.

Throughout the years, Victoria learned the ways of Japan by learning their language, customs, and traditions. As a child, she enjoyed riding to school each day with Mrs. Izumi and eventually became one of her students. Over the years, the bond between Victoria and the Izumi family grew stronger. Victoria also continued to exchange letters with The Lady in Pink and share life experiences.

Eventually, Victoria became an elementary school teacher where Mrs. Izumi once taught before retirement. Victoria received a *Teacher of the Year* award for her outstanding contributions in meeting the needs of students with learning and physical disabilities. She later married a gentleman named, Joe, a math teacher in the school where she worked. Years later, Victoria received an unexpected letter from The Lady in Pink. After reading it, she, without hesitation, left for Stillwaters.

Caroline's Adoption Journey

Caroline and her new adoptive family arrived at port after journeying from Stillwaters' Orphanage. Jim politely carried Caroline's luggage on board the ship as she trailed holding hands with Betty. Once on board, Betty and Caroline went to their designated room and Jim entered into another room next to theirs.

"Here's a new dress for you. I thought you might want to put it on as we prepare for brunch on the upper deck," said Betty.

Caroline excitedly took the dress and changed into it, saying, "Thank you, it's pretty and has flowers on it."

"You're welcome, my dear." The adjoined door between the two rooms opened and Jim walked into Betty's and Caroline's room wearing a nice three-piece brown striped suit.

"Honey, you look quite dashing," said Betty.

"You look lovely and beautiful as well my darling. Caroline, you too."

"I believe we're ready to attend the brunch. This way, my dears," said Jim graciously.

As they dined during the evening, men of prestige and high social status entered the dining area wearing tuxedos and bow ties.

The tables were all elegantly decorated with the finest white table linen, gold porcelain china, gold silverware, gold napkin rings with personalized embroidered silk napkins and gold rimmed glassware suitable for dignitaries. Soon, classical music of Mozart, Beethoven, Bernstein and Gershwin set the tone. "That's the same music that The Lady in Pink would play for us," Caroline said.

"So, you have heard this music before?" asked Jim.

"Yes."

"I am impressed, Caroline. Perhaps you would like to dance with me?"

"Yes, but I'm too little and can't reach up that high," Caroline said.

"It's okay, I will just reach down and hold your hands." As Jim danced with Caroline, the crowd began to cheer for them as they pranced instep. Betty smiled, slightly teary-eyed as she stared at the father and daughter bonding. She could bear no children of her own but gratefully accepted Caroline as her first child.

"This is fun, and I can turn around too," Caroline giggled, smiling.

"You are a really good dancer."

"You too, Mr. Jim."

Soon the music came to an end, dinner concluded, and everyone tucked in for the night. Throughout the rest of the journey, they all became acquainted and continued to have fun by going up on the ship's deck to observe dolphins splashing about in the ocean.

After a few days of sailing, they arrive at the port in New York.

"Look at the big, lady statue," Caroline said.

"Yes, that's the Statue of Liberty and it symbolizes American freedom," said Betty.

"I want to see it. Can we go there one day?"

"Of course, dear," responded Betty.

On their way home, Caroline was overcome with the excitement of the tall buildings and seeing the fashionable mannequins in the store windows. "I want that dress and want to look like her. Do you think I'm pretty too?"

"You are gorgeous, and who knows, you may want to be in the fashion business like us—If you want, of course," said Jim. Finally, they arrived home and Caroline looked up at the tall skyscraper building as she was about to enter. "Is this my new home?"

"Yes," said Betty.

"Who is that man and why is he dressed like that?"

"He's a doorman, and he will help us take our luggage inside. You will get used to it," said Jim, chuckling.

After unpacking and showing Caroline her room, they took her sightseeing. She visited Broadway, the Statue of Liberty and many shopping stores.

As time went on, Caroline attended the most prestigious private elementary school in New York, where she enjoyed sketching and drawing. Upon entering high school, Caroline began her amateur modeling career. She and The Lady in Pink continued to write letters, sharing life experiences.

After graduation, Caroline was accepted at New York University where she studied fashion designing. Upon successfully completing her studies in the university, Caroline became a fashion designer and modeled for several retail chains.

While working and traveling, Caroline began experiencing unfamiliar symptoms but overlooked them. There were sudden periods of temporary vision loss in one of her eyes, extreme tiredness and unfamiliar tingling sensations in her hands. She even had trouble walking at times but thought she was working too much. She took some time off to see if that would help and found relief, but the symptoms kept returning. She informed Jim and Betty, who later brought in doctors to treat her, but none of them could find the root cause of the symptoms.

Years later, Caroline, now in her early thirties, received a concerning letter from The Lady in Pink. She quickly packed and rushed to the orphanage as fast as she could.

Marilyn's Adoption Journey

As Maria and Marilyn ventured by taxi towards the North Georgia Mountains, the newly adopted orphan held her new poodle and slept the entire journey. "We're home Marilyn, you can bring Shakespeare inside and I will take your luggage."

"Thank you." Maria opened the door and as they entered, a banner with Marilyn's name was displayed in the foyer of the house that read, "Welcome Home, Marilyn." Maria then asked Marilyn, "Do you like the banner."

"I love it. Did you make it for me?"

"I sure did, and Shakespeare helped me too. Marilyn, let me show you to your room," Maria said.

Maria guided Marilyn to her bedroom and as they entered, Marilyn yelled, "Wow! I love the big yellow Teddy Bear."

"I am glad you like it. Shakespeare can sleep in here with you. There's his bed in the corner."

"I am so happy that he's going to be with me," Marilyn said kissing Shakespeare.

"I'm glad you're here and since we have had such a long ride, I will let you rest a bit," said Maria.

"Okay." Marilyn climbed into the bed and fell asleep with Shakespeare cuddled in her arms.

Hours passed, and Maria went into the room. "Marilyn, it's time for dinner. Let me show you where to wash your hands."

"Thank you."

"I hope you like spaghetti and meatballs," Maria said.

"Yes, ma'am."

They entered the kitchen and sat near each other. Maria began serving dinner and Marilyn looked on. "This looks and smells good."

"Yes, it's my favorite dish."

"Sorry, Shakespeare, you can't eat this. Can we say the blessing?" Marilyn asked.

"That would be delightful Marilyn, please begin when you are ready."

"Lord, bless Maria, Shakespeare, Ms. Lady and my friends, and the food, Amen."

"Thank you for the blessing."

"You're welcome. The Lady in Pink showed us," Marilyn said.

"She did a great job with you all. I'm proud of you."

"Thank you."

"Well, tell me what else did you learn while you were with The Lady in Pink."

"Well, I learned how to fight and forgive."

Maria stopped eating, looked at Marilyn in confusion, and asked, "Did you say *fight*?"

"Yes, that's how I lost my tooth. Katherine hit me, so I hit her back. We apologized and forgave each other," Marilyn said.

"What happened?"

"We got into an argument after she stepped on my foot. I pushed her, pulled her hair and tore Katherine's dress. She tore mine first."

"Okay, what did you learn from that lesson?"

"Um, I think a man named The Lord wants us to love and not fight each other. Oh, and not to lie either."

Maria chuckled and said, "Well, that's true and the right way to fight is in the courts."

"What's a *courts*?" Marilyn asked.

"It's a place where people settle arguments without hitting each other. As a lawyer, I argue the right way and fight for the rights of others without using my hands. A judge or people help to decide the cases."

"Can I be a Law-er?" asked Marilyn

"Maybe one day you will be one, but you must learn how to control yourself," Maria said.

The next few years, Marilyn enjoyed attending elementary school, making friends and spending time with Shakespeare. She and The Lady in Pink maintained contact and wrote to each other frequently. As she entered her teens, Marilyn began fighting and arguing with other students to prove her point. She was suspended from school and received numerous consequences. However, she did form a bond with a counselor named, Arabella, who took a special interest in her and established a close relationship that lasted throughout her high school years. Maria really struggled to get her on track throughout her teenage years and often questioned whether to send her back to the orphanage.

After her high school graduation, Marilyn continued to get into trouble and was eventually sent to a youth conversion center for troubled youth. She began to read books on practicing law and reviewing case laws. Whenever she got into trouble, she appealed her case using case law precedents. The director of the youth conversion center met with Maria and discussed getting Marilyn into law school. At that point, Maria was exhausted with trying to convince Marilyn to stay out of trouble.

Eventually, Marilyn was released and begged Maria to help her get into college to study law. Seeing Marilyn's desire and perseverance to pursue her interest, Maria supported her in going to college. Marilyn went on to successfully complete college where she studied Labor Laws; her passion grew for protecting the rights of employees and children. She then became one of the very few women of Georgia to pass the bar exam and licensed to practice law. The Lady in Pink and the other former orphans traveled to Marilyn's graduation, celebrating her momentous success.

After graduation, Marilyn used her skills and knowledge to fight against oppressive child labor and unfair minimum wages. Marilyn later married a lawyer named Conley, whom she fell in love with from the law firm she worked at. They both shared the love of raising a wonderful baby boy named Bo. Until one unfortunate day, Marilyn and her husband suffered the devasting loss of their infant son. Bo tragically lost his life when he fell out of his high chair and hit his head on the floor. After baby Bo's death, Marilyn and Conley's marriage struggled severely for many years, eventually causing them to divorce.

After the divorce, Marilyn's life became increasingly difficult to manage and she became dependent on medications to suppress the pain. Thus, leading to dependency that caused her to spiral out of control with anger and deep depression. Her adoptive mother, Maria, tried to support her, but Marilyn's anger issues drove her away. She never shared her loss with anyone from the orphanage home, until one day, she decided to write a letter to Katherine, informing her of the tragedies she endured, and also requesting support to get her life back together. Without hesitation, Katherine sent a letter to Marilyn stating that she'd come and support her through the crisis. Almost three weeks later, there was a knock at the door. Marilyn peeked outside the window and became excited when she saw that Katherine was standing outside the door. Marilyn opened the door and hugged and greeted Katherine.

"Come in. You look great Katherine," Marilyn said.

"You do too, and I love your hat," Katherine replied.

"Let me show you to your room. This way."

"You have a lovely home."

"Thank you, I moved here after the divorce."

"I'm so very sorry, Marilyn," Katherine said tenderly.

After settling in, they both enjoyed a meal and reminisced about childhood memories of Stillwaters' Orphanage and about the infamous fight that took place. Throughout the next several days, Marilyn continued to battle depression.

"I don't like who I am and it's all my fault. I should have been a better wife and mother," cried Marilyn.

"We can't change the past or be afraid of the future. You must take it one day at a time. Let God control the things you can't change," Katherine said to Marilyn, trying to comfort her.

"Katherine, what do you know of pain and suffering? You were lucky to get adopted into a rich family who provided everything for you. I have worked for everything and now I have lost it all. Don't sit there and act all pious," Marilyn said in anger.

"My word, I am not going to sit here and let you take your anger out on me. I am here because you asked me to come. I will not allow you to make me your doormat," Katherine said sternly while heading to the front door.

After Katherine's comment, Marilyn, without out warning, took her red, high heel shoe off of her right foot and stared angrily at Katherine as she was leaving.

"You wouldn't dare throw that at me. Marilyn, what is wrong with you? You're like a wild beast." Katherine was confused and shocked at how fast the situation escalated.

Marilyn didn't respond as she stared upon Katherine with rage, still aiming the red shoe at her. Katherine saw the crazed look in her friend's eyes and then said in a calm voice, "Look Marilyn, I know you've been through a lot but—" Katherine's sentence was interrupted as Marilyn, unexpectantly, hurled the shoe at Katherine as hard as she could, striking her opponent in the shoulder. Katherine quickly grabbed a broom by the front door, ran towards Marilyn, and took a wild swing. The sound of whooshing wind could be heard from the forceful swing and then a cracking sound as the broomstick connected on top of Marilyn's head, immediately causing her to drop to the floor.

"Oh my, Marilyn, please wake up, I'm so sorry. I don't know what overcame me," Katherine panicked.

Unresponsive but breathing, Marilyn laid motionless on the floor as Katherine rushed to the kitchen to get cold water.

Katherine returned to her unconscious friend and doused water from a bowl onto her face. Marilyn lifted her head gasping as if she was drowning while spitting and looking dazed. When Marilyn lifted her head, her hat fell off and that's when Katherine noticed the baldness on top of her friend's head.

Marilyn looked around the house trying to gather her bearings and asked, "What happened? How did I get on the floor? Where is my shoe? I can't remember anything."

"You really need help. Let's get you to a doctor. What happened to your hair?" asked Katherine in a concerned tone.

"I don't want to talk about it. I'm alright. Just get me to the bed."

Katherine assisted Marilyn to her room and helped her climb into bed. Katherine decided to lay alongside her orphan sister with sadness and guilt from the troublesome event. "I am sorry. Will you forgive me?" Katherine asked apologetically.

"For what?"

"Well, I hit you with a broom after you hit me with your shoe," Katherine stated.

"My Katherine, you really should watch your temper," snickered Marilyn.

"My temper?!" yelled Katherine, chuckling a bit, "You were waving your shoe around like a deranged lunatic!" she continued.

"If I don't remember it—it never happened," laughed Marilyn, rubbing her head. "Anyways, I guess I can forgive you. I'm sorry as well."

"I can't believe we fought as if we were children again," Katherine said while smiling.

"Me neither, let's both get some much-needed rest," Marilyn laughed.

"Oh, I forgot to tell you something," said Katherine.

"What is it, Katherine?"

"I won! Again!" Katherine playfully celebrated.

"No, you're just a cheat as always," Marilyn defended while grinning at Katherine.

Marilyn then scanned Katherine's hand and said, "Why are you not married yet? Are you too much of a pain to be bothered with?"

Katherine rolled her eyes and explained, "If you must know, I met a wonderful man named Makembi. He's a doctor, who truly adores children. We've worked together for a few years caring for sick children in Africa. He recently started courting me. We are still getting to know each other, I suppose."

Marilyn looked at Katherine and said, "Sorry for bringing you into my troubled life. You should be with him instead of me."

Katherine bent down and moved her mouth closer to Marilyn's ear, and then she whispered, "I know your secret—You're not sorry. You just want me to stay with you and no one else for forever and ever." They both burst into laughter. Soon after, the former orphans fell asleep.

Being the first to awake later in the evening, Katherine awakened Marilyn.

"Why are you waking me up?" Marilyn mumbled, struggling to wake up.

"I have something important to ask you."

"Katherine, what is it?" responded Marilyn, clearly agitated and groggy from being awakened.

"I was thinking, after all you have been through, a change of environment and a whole new life may be just what you need," suggested Katherine.

She then asked with a grin, "Marilyn, would you like to come back to Africa with me and volunteer, helping children in orphanages?"

"Katherine, I would love that, how soon can I come? I just need to get out of this town. It holds so many terrible memories for me."

"It's up to you, Marilyn."

"Let's start packing tomorrow."

"Tomorrow?" questioned Katherine with shock and excitement in her voice.

"Katherine, the sooner the better for me."

The next day, they both packed and began their journey to Katherine's home, Africa.

Katherine's Adoption Journey

A promise is a promise, Katherine said quietly to herself as she journeyed with Ma'am Kizi from Stillwaters. She stared into the sky and noticed a dove flying above her carriage.

Once they arrived at port, Katherine noticed that they were walking to ship that didn't have a long line of people boarding. In fact, Ma'am Kizi, her family, staff, and Katherine were the only people boarding this particular ship. Once they all boarded the ship, Ma'am Kizi and Katherine enjoyed a restful moment of relaxing before dining. After several hours of rest, everyone gathered in the ship's dining area for a meal.

"Katherine, what can I get for you?"

"I like chicken and cornbread. Just like The Lady in Pink cooked."

"As you wish," Ma'am Kizi replied with a smile. Ma'am Kizi's servants prepared dinner and set the table onboard the ship. After dinner was served at the table and everyone sat, Ma'am Kizi asked Katherine, "What do you like to do?"

"I like to help people get well. I tried to help my grandma, but she died," Katherine said.

"Well one day, you're going to help a lot of people."

Katherine started to look around the ship and then she asked Ma'am Kizi, "Why are we the only people on this big ship?"

Ma'am Kizi winked and simply responded, "It's so you can run around and play until your heart is content, my dear." Ma'am Kizi didn't feel the need to explain the advantages of being wealthy and royal at that moment.

After several weeks of sailing, they finally arrive in Africa.

"Look at the elephant, it is big," Katherine said.

"This is where they live, and you will see lots of them throughout your life here in Nigeria. I will teach you more about our ways here in Africa. Also, since you want to help people, you can start here—and maybe even become a great doctor someday," Ma'am Kizi said.

"No, I want to help children at an orphanage like The Lady in Pink."

Ma'am Kizi smiled and said, "I will support you in anything you want to do in life, dear."

Over the years, Katherine learned the customs, traditions and ways of Africa. She attended school, made friends and learned the ways of her notable wealthy family. As she grew into her teens, Ma'am Kizi began to introduce more spirituality into Katherine's life.

"This is my sister, Susanna, who travels all around Africa, teaching people about the bible and the power of prayer." Katherine enjoyed learning from Ma'am Kizi's sister, Susanna, and they began working together in the village orphanage. While at the orphanage, Katherine and Susanna cared for sick, abused, and abandoned children.

Katherine continued her educational journey into high school, where she made many more friends who joined her in volunteering at the local orphanages. Katherine occasionally wrote and shared her experiences as a volunteer with The Lady in Pink. Katherine continued living her passion by traveling around different villages in Africa and providing aid.

During her tenure, she developed feelings for a local doctor, Makembi, who provided medical care for the children in the orphanages. The two had just begun to court until Katherine received a letter from Marilyn describing the loss of her child Bo and the divorce from her husband that followed. The letter requested her support due to the increasing crisis that Marilyn was experiencing. She immediately boarded a ship and set sail to tend to her childhood friend. Upon arrival, Katherine encountered many struggles in supporting Marilyn and insisted that she come back to Africa with her to volunteer in the orphanages. After Marilyn agreed, they traveled to Africa and Katherine found that the experience was life-changing for her hurting friend. Finding peace in providing comfort to children at orphanages, Marilyn eventually decided to make Africa her permanent home. She continued to wear her hats whenever in public, not wanting her hair loss to be questioned again. Marilyn started going to local doctors alone because she was worried, not only about the hair loss, but also her weight loss. Even though Katherine was concerned, she respected Marilyn's privacy.

Years later, Katherine and Marilyn received devastating letters from The Lady in Pink that brought much sadness to their hearts. The Lady in Pink wrote letters to all of her former orphans, and in the letter addressed to Katherine, the last line read, *"Katherine, never forget your promise."*

After receiving letters from their former caretaker, Katherine and Marilyn boarded a ship to journey back to Stillwaters.

PART II:

JOURNEYS

¹*To everything there is a season, and a time to every purpose under the heaven:*

²*A time to be born, and a time to die; a time to plant, and a time to pluck up that which is planted;*

⁴*A time to weep, and a time to laugh; a time to mourn, and a time to dance*

(Ecclesiastes 3:1-2,4 KJV)

CHAPTER FIVE

DEVASTATING NEWS AT STILLWATERS

*A*s The Lady's letters were received by the former orphans, each one of them journeyed back to the orphanage in hopes of seeing and caring for their loving guardian, The Lady in Pink.

Meanwhile, The Lady was battling a life-threatening condition and wasn't sure that she would be alive by the time the women all returned to the orphanage, so she gave instructions to her doctor, Dr. Stinson, in event of her passing. The Lady told the doctor to take her body away to be preserved and to bury her only once all of the former orphans arrived back to the orphanage. She also told him to have her buried under The Cherry Blossom Tree and to reside over the orphanage until one of the former orphans returned.

The doctor agreed to The Lady in Pink's terms. Almost two weeks later, Caroline, the first of the orphans to arrive back to Stillwaters' Orphanage, came through the unlocked backdoor mentioned in The Lady's letter. When Caroline walked in, she saw a man sitting at the kitchen table, reading a newspaper.

"Hello, who are you?" Caroline inquired, wondering who the man was.

"Hello, my name is Dr. Stinson. I hate to tell you this, but I have some very unfortunate news I have to share with you. You may want to sit down, ma'am." expressed Dr. Stinson in a soft tone.

Caroline sat down at the kitchen table with the doctor, and he sadly explained to her that The Lady in Pink had passed earlier that morning. After the news, the doctor consoled and monitored Caroline for a few hours. Later, he told her of The Lady's last wishes before he got up to leave.

"Oh, I almost forgot, Caroline, there are fresh foods and supplies here from the local market for you and the others once they arrived. It is the least I could do, and I will be checking in with the family periodically," Dr. Stinson assured.

Caroline thanked the doctor as he left, but she was now troubled by her new task of having to deliver the grim message of The Lady in Pink's death to the other fellow orphans as they arrived back to the house.

Three days after Caroline's arrival, Reba arrived from France. Two days after Reba's arrival, Victoria arrived from Japan. Lastly, Marilyn and Katherine returned from Africa four days after Victoria. All of the women, now back at their once safe haven, were grieving and consoling one another from the shock of The Lady in Pink's death. Days before the graveside memorial service, they all shared memories of their times at the Stillwaters' Orphanage. They cried and laughed as they browsed through The Lady's personal diary, detailing their arrivals, personalities, loss, struggles, fights, funny moments, the Cleotus and Rosey moment, adoptions, travels, celebrations, and her own personal struggles.

"Let's go through some of the closets," Marilyn said.

The women all reminisced as they held up the little dresses that The Lady in Pink kept of them as orphans.

"Wow, I can't believe she saved the dresses that we fought in," said Katherine.

"Me either!" replied Marilyn looking at the torn lace collar, laughing.

"I love your fight story," Victoria said laughing.

"I do too, I wish I was there to have seen The Lady's reaction," laughed Reba.

Marilyn walked back to the closet to hang her torn childhood dress, "You know, Katherine and I are simply friends and enemies at the same time. It's just how it goes, and no one knows why. We love each other in our own special way and that's all that matters, I suppose."

"It's good to see that you two are getting along and staying in the same country," Caroline said.

Only if she knew, thought Katherine to herself.

"Look, it's The Lady in Pink's favorite long dress with the pink blossoms. She was so graceful, and just the perfect *lady*," Reba said as she looked through the closet.

Victoria quickly grabbed the dress out of the closet before Reba did and said, "Yes, she was the complete opposite of you, Reba." Reba frowned and playfully shoved Victoria for the making the comment. Victoria laughed and then suggested, "Hey! Let's see who can fit into the dress. Marilyn, you can try it on first."

Marilyn took the dress from Victoria and tried it on but had a hard time sliding it down past her waist. Eventually, she gave up, took off the dress, and said, "I got to start exercising. Caroline, your turn."

Caroline took the dress from Marilyn and measured it to her body, without putting it on. She then said, "I'll pass, I don't want to look foolish like Marilyn. Reba, are you brave enough to try? Here, it's your turn."

Reba put on the dress and it almost fit perfectly but the sleeves were too tight. "Did she have twigs for arms," Reba said in frustration, "Help me take it off, Victoria! This was your grand idea!" Victoria helped Reba squeeze out of the dress.

"Since I am the most beautiful lady here, I will surely have no problems at all," Victoria assured in a condescending tone to the other women as she slowly tried on the dress. Halfway through Victoria trying to squeeze into the dress, she suddenly panicked, "I can't breathe!" The women burst into laughter as they watched Victoria struggle to put on the dress. "Don't just stand there, help me take it off!" yelled Victoria. Katherine sarcastically responded, "Okay, okay, ladies. Let's help the most beautiful lady take off the dress." They all helped take the dress off Victoria.

Victoria was out of breath from struggling to take off the dress and then she said to Katherine, "Here Katherine, you try it on. Let's see how much luck you'll have."

Katherine tried on the dress. "It's a perfect fit! I love it! Maybe one day, I will wear it again. Let me get out of it and hang it in my closet," Katherine said.

"Your perfect little body annoys me to no end, Katherine," joked Marilyn.

"Hey, let's go into the kitchen area and see if she saved our poetry plates," said Caroline excitedly.

As they made their way into the kitchen, the women noticed that the furniture remained the same as it was when they arrived as children.

"She hasn't changed a thing and even the old rocking chair is still in the living room. Let's go inside and look around. I can still remember screaming and yelling for my mother," said Caroline, tearing up.

"I can remember arriving here after losing my grandmother and had no idea where I would end up. It was terrifying—You know, I still remember the fight Marilyn and I had in here," Katherine said while starting to laugh.

Marilyn laughed and said to Katherine, "I am still embarrassed by the way we pretended to faint during dinner when she got up to look inside the living room at the mess we made. It was terrible but funny."

"We were absolutely horrid at times, but The Lady in Pink showed us how important love was over material things, arguments and fights when she cleaned up our mess. She even left us a letter with candy afterward after our brawl. She taught us all the meaning of forgiveness and love," said Katherine.

Victoria interrupted the conversation, "If you two were my children, I don't know if I would have been as kind as The Lady. I would have saved myself the trouble and just locked you two into separate rooms for eternity."

Marilyn sarcastically responded, "Thank you for your input, Victoria. Oh, and please never do anything that requires an act of kindness, why, it may cause your tiny heart to break into little, black pieces and the world would just be *so* devasted, could you imagine?" The other women burst into laughter after hearing Marilyn's comments, Victoria immediately gave everyone a dirty look, but eventually joined in the laughter herself. After the humor died down a bit, Marilyn continued and said, "I can remember it all felt like a dream when I escaped my mother's beatings. I was always hungry and never knew when my next meal would come, until I came here. I was even afraid of The Lady in Pink until she held me. I still remember her warmth. From then on, I knew I was safe," Marilyn said crying. Everyone embraced her for the moment before reminiscing further.

"I remember singing and dancing when they took me away from my stepfather. I felt like a bird being released from a cage for the first time. The orphanage was my first real home. I am sure we all can remember The Lady in Pink's biscuits, eggs, bacon and syrup. Not to mention how good her Cherry Blossom Cream Cheese Muffins were. She was the best cook in the world," Reba said. They all nodded and smiled at each other in agreement.

"I can remember coming here angry and calling everyone Rolly Polly eyes," Victoria chuckled a bit, with her eyes fixated on the floor. "I was so angry when my father passed, now that I think about it, I was actually mad at him because he said he would return. I was an only child and he raised me as his best friend and daughter. My whole world had fallen apart but The Lady in Pink and everyone in this room became my family. I am forever grateful to The Lady in Pink. We should all cherish these memories and continue to honor her memory by being there for one another," said Victoria crying. The women nodded in agreement again and paused while staring at The Lady in Pink's rocking chair with her favorite books stacked on the floor.

One by one, they all kissed the chair and sobbed as they passed by in respect of her legacy heading towards the kitchen. A solemn mood created an atmosphere of bereavement as they sat in their favorite kitchen chairs.

"Everything about the orphanage seems much smaller now that we have grown older. I can still see our names handwritten in pink on the back of the chairs," said Caroline. "Let me get the poetry dishes. I believe they are in this cupboard." Caroline searched up and down the cupboard, "I don't see them," she said, scratching her head. Caroline then went and searched another cupboard, "Ah, here they are," said Reba, with relief.

She handed out The Lady in Pink's engraved poetry plates individually designed with poems for each of the women when they were orphan children. Marilyn picked up her plate and began reading the engraved writing in a soft tone, *"With kisses and hugs, I can snuggle like a bug."*

Reba followed, *"With happiness and cheers, I can chase away my fears."*

Next was Katherine, *"As the moon brightens each midnight sky, so does the sun for each tear I cry."*

"Oh, me, me, me!" yelled Caroline. The women burst into laughter. After the laughter subdued, Caroline cited, *"No matter how heavy my heart may be, I can always find love underneath the Cherry Blossom Tree."*

Victoria then stared at her plate teary-eyed for several seconds, and then softly read, *"Let peace be still to one and all, no matter how great, no matter how small."*

The kitchen became silent as everyone sat quietly in solemn respect. Later in the day, they prepared dinner and tucked in for the night. Katherine chose to stay in The Lady in Pink's room. After Katherine dressed for bed, she curiously walked over to a tall, dark brown dresser in The Lady's room and opened the middle drawer. Inside the drawer were sketched pictures of each of them as orphans. As everyone slept, she went by the other former orphan's rooms, leaving a picture by each door. "Hmm, I wonder what happened to Cleotus and Rosey. I hope they come to the memorial service tomorrow," Katherine said to herself smiling.

The next morning, each of the women arose and shared their love for the sketches that were left as a surprise by Katherine.

"Hey, when were these sketches made? We are all little girls in these pictures," Caroline questioned to the group.

"Who knows, The Lady in Pink was a true lady of many talents," replied Reba.

Afterwards, they all ate breakfast and took a local carriage into town to complete arrangements for The Lady in Pink's memorial service to be held the next day. While in town, they ran into

Clergyman Madison who then introduced them to The Lady's doctor, Dr. Stinson. "Hello everyone, and hello again Caroline, I'm happy to finally meet you all," expressed Dr. Stinson. The clergyman and the doctor spoke highly of The Lady in Pink and gave the women their condolences while promising to attend her service. After the gentlemen left, the women all chose to browse the town stores and purchase additional accessories to go along with their attire before taking the carriage back to the orphanage.

As soon as the women arrived at the orphanage, Katherine stepped down from the carriage and started walking towards the Cherry Blossom Tree where they played as little girls, the other women trailed behind her. "This will be her new home," said Katherine with a sigh. She then started tying a pink bow on a wooden stake marking The Lady in Pink's final resting place. Everyone stood in silence for a few moments, reflecting on the memories of their loving childhood with the caretaker.

Victoria broke the silence by saying, "It's getting dark now, let's make our way inside and make supper." They all left with heavy hearts as they return to the orphanage. Dinner was especially quiet on this night, as they all thought about the funeral that was taking place the next day. After dinner, they all quickly turned in for the night.

The next morning, no one wanted breakfast as they got dressed for the memorial service. As the service time drew near, everyone made their way to the gravesite underneath the Cherry Blossom Tree. Soon the carriage appeared in the distance coming toward the orphanage with The Lady's pink draped coffin. Clergyman Madison, Dr. Stinson, Cleotus, Rosey and few others from town arrived showing their respect for her legacy and contributions. As the service began, Clergyman Madison paid tribute to The Lady in Pink by highlighting her many contributions to the community and orphanage services. He conducted the eulogy with a prayer and ceremonial tribute. "Will each of the women who were orphans here place a pink blossom on top of the coffin?" The clergyman asked while giving each a blossom. All of the former Stillwaters' orphans stepped forward one by one, placing the flower on The Lady in Pink's coffin with tears flowing amongst them all.

"May she forever rest in peace," said Clergyman Madison, as he concluded the eulogy holding his bible up to the sky.

After the eulogy, The Stillwaters' women got together and went over to the Cherry Blossom Tree and, one at a time carved the letters "Lady in Pink" into it. Marilyn was last to carve into the tree, and as she started, a white dove unexpectedly descended from the treetop and flew near her head, causing her to duck from being startled. As the dove flew away, it began to coo loudly. Then, all of a sudden, Marilyn collapsed to the ground and gripped her stomach in pain. "Help! Help me! Help me! It hurts so bad!" screamed Marilyn.

The women ran over to Marilyn's aid. After approaching her and kneeling beside her, they notice the baldness of her head. Marilyn's pink hat had fallen off as she collapsed to the ground. They all looked at one another with confusion and worry.

Marilyn laid motionless and weak as they all tried to comfort her. "It's going to be alright. Dr. Stinson! Dr. Stinsooon! Uh, I believe I saw him walking towards the carriage. Someone get him now! Please!" ordered Katherine frantically, as she held Marilyn's hand and looked around for Dr. Stinson. Caroline and Reba got up to search for the doctor.

Dr. Stinson heard faint shouting as he was about to climb onto Clergyman Madison's carriage. He looked back and witnessed everyone gathering around a person lying on the ground. The doctor and the clergyman climbed off the carriage and ran to the scene.

"Oh my Dr. Stinson, we were looking for you. I am so glad you're here, I don't know what happened, she just fell," Katherine said moving back, frantically. Dr. Stinson moved in and put his ear near Marilyn's mouth to listen to her breathing. Marilyn then started coughing up blood.

"Help me get her inside the house," Dr. Stinson said to Clergyman Madison.

Together they gently picked up Marilyn from the ground and started walking towards the orphanage.

"You will be alright, my dear," comforted Dr. Stinson while walking and helping to carry her inside the orphanage.

Once the men got Marilyn inside, Katherine said to them, "Place her in this bedroom. She will be most comfortable here."

While lying her on the bed, Marilyn suddenly started hysterically yelling, "Mama No! Please don't hit me! I promise that it wasn't my fault. I want my baby "Bo" back!" Dr. Stinson gave her various medicines to help her sleep. "Just let her rest for now and I will come back to check on her tomorrow. It's so peculiar, she seemed fine earlier… Maybe the funeral triggered something? Regardless, the real concern is the hair loss and the blood, so I will do some research tonight to see what it could be," Dr. Stinson said to the women.

Just before leaving, Clergyman Madison offered a word of prayer as the women all bowed their heads. *"Father, God of heaven and earth, grant comfort during Marilyn's time of illness. Amen."* Both Dr. Stinson and Clergyman Madison wished everyone a good day as they left the orphanage.

Katherine and Caroline remained at Marilyn's bedside throughout the night to tend to Marilyn, while the others slept. "I feel we all need to remain here for a few days to make sure she is going to be okay. I'm also going to send a letter to Maria to see if she knows what is going on with her," whispered Katherine.

"I agree, why wouldn't she tell us that she was losing hair?" whispered back Caroline, hoping not to wake Marilyn. "Would you have told us if you were in her situation?" questioned Katherine. Caroline didn't respond and they both just sat quietly on Marilyn's bed and stared at her as she slept. "You can get some rest and I'll stay with her." Caroline got up and kissed Katherine on the cheek before heading to her room.

Early the next morning, there was a knock at the door. Reba peeked through the window and saw that it was Dr. Stinson. She rushed to open the door, "Good Morning Dr. Stinson."

"Good morning, Reba. I came back to check on Marilyn. How did she sleep last night?" Dr. Stinson asked.

"Katherine said that Marilyn had a very restless night. She was tossing, turning, and hallucinating," replied Reba. Concerned about Marilyn's health, Dr. Stinson entered her room. He stopped by her bed, pulled up a chair and checked her pulse.

"Good morning, dear. I came by to check on you. How are you feeling today?" Dr. Stinson asked with a slight smile.

"I'm fine. Um, who are you, again?" Marilyn puzzled.

"My name is Dr. Stinson, and I treated you after you fainted underneath the Cherry Blossom Tree yesterday. Do you remember fainting?"

"I don't remember anything other than feeling pain," Marilyn groaned.

After checking Marilyn's health, Dr. Stinson appeared concerned. "After doing some research last night, I am afraid you have symptoms related to cancer. You have significant hair loss and you lost quite a bit of blood yesterday, so I'm going to start a blood infusion today. Have you experienced significant weight loss?"

"Maybe."

"Have you been to the doctor recently?"

"Yes."

"What did he say about your health?"

"To be honest, Dr. Stinson, I was told months ago that I was in the last stage of cancer with no cure."

"Marilyn, I am going to fight for you and with you. I will start you on a series of aggressive medicines to help fight this illness. I just need you to keep fighting."

"Dr. Stinson, she has suffered the loss of her husband and son. She's my sister and I can't lose her," Katherine cried holding Marilyn's hand.

After hearing Dr. Stinson's grim diagnosis, Katherine rushed out of the room crying and called for the other women. "Victoria! Reba! Caroline! Can you all come inside and close the door?" They all rushed to Marilyn's bedside. "Dr. Stinson has something to share with you all."

"Good morning ladies, there is no easy way to say this but, Marilyn's health is rapidly declining, but we are going to put up a fight as long as we can. I just need you all to fight with us and remain positive," said Dr. Stinson, wanting to give the women hope.

Upon hearing that, the women began to slowly sit on both sides of Marilyn's bed, embracing her and crying.

Dr. Stinson gently squeezed Marilyn's hand. "You will not fight this alone. We are fighting with you," he said before exiting the room.

As Dr. Stinson was walking out the door, Clergyman Madison was walking towards the house to check on Marilyn. The doctor updated Clergyman Madison on Marilyn's condition. After conversing with Dr. Stinson, the clergyman cleared his throat loudly to let everyone inside know that he was present.

"We're in Katherine's room," said Victoria.

Clergyman Madison walked in the room and said, "I just talked with Dr. Stinson and he looked a bit sad, but I believe—" He then stopped mid-sentence as he looked around at the sad faces of the women. He looked down at Marilyn and calmly asked, "How are you doing, my child?"

"I am going to be okay. I am a fighter," Marilyn said weakly.

A loud sigh escaped Clergyman Madison as he kneeled beside Marilyn's bed, praying, "*Father, grant Marilyn comfort from her pain, peace from her fears and wipe away all of her tears. Amen.*" Clergyman Madison stood up and patted Marilyn's hands gently. Before Clergyman Madison left the orphanage, he whispered to the women that he will be praying for them before exiting.

No one wanted to eat breakfast or lunch after hearing the report. Later that afternoon, the sad, former orphans decided to prepare dinner and eat out of the poetry plates. Each of them reached inside the old cupboard for their favorite poetry plate and carried Marilyn's plate to her bedside. They all sat alongside her, eating and sharing memories and stories of each other's lives. As the evening approached, Victoria, Caroline and Reba all prepared dinner. Katherine refused to leave Marilyn's side. "You know, when you became the first female lawyer to become a Georgia Supreme Court judge, I knew it was right for you. You have always felt you had the last word no matter how we argued and fought," Katherine said laughing.

Marilyn laughed out loud, "You're right and I never thought about it until now."

Several days passed, and everyone's goal was to make sure that Marilyn was comfortable. One afternoon, there was a knock at the door. Caroline opened the door and a lady nervously said, "Hello, I'm Maria, Marilyn's adoptive mother, I received a letter from Katherine and came as fast as I could."

Caroline welcomed her inside and said, "She is going to be so happy to see you. Follow me this way." Caroline led Maria to Marilyn and when they walked into the room Marilyn excitedly said, "Maria! It's you."

Maria entered the room hugging Katherine as she made her way to Marilyn's bedside.

Marilyn reached out and grabbed Maria's hand and asked, "How did you know I was here?"

"Katherine sent me a letter about your condition."

"Thank you, Katherine."

"Anything for my sister and friend. Maria, why don't I take your things for you? I will show you to your room later."

"No, I believe I'll stay right here alongside my Marilyn if that's alright."

"Of course, Maria. It looks like you're going to have a room full, Marilyn, and I will be here as well," Katherine said smiling. "I will give you two some alone time and I will be back later."

"Thank you again, Katherine," Maria gratefully responded as Katherine exited the room.

"Marilyn, I regret every day how I left you alone when you needed me most. I find it hard to forgive myself when I know there were times you needed me."

"Stop blaming yourself, Maria. It wasn't you that made bad choices—it was me. And, I take full responsibility for them. I pushed away the very people I needed when my baby died. I even blamed my husband and drove him away. I hurt the very ones I loved the most, even you, the greatest mother I could have asked for."

"Marilyn, I hope you can forgive me."

"Oh, Maria, it is me that should be asking you for forgiveness. *I* sincerely apologize for my actions back then,"

"I forgive you and never stopped loving you," said Maria

"Thank you for your love and coming to help me fight this."

"Fight what?" questioned Maria to Marilyn.

"I have had cancer for some years and tried to hide it. But now it's aggressive and I don't know if…" Marilyn stopped and sobbed. Maria hugged her and cried, "Can you help me up?" Marilyn reached for Maria as she trembled while standing to her feet.

"Marilyn, where are you going? You are too weak."

"Take me to the Cherry Blossom Tree where The Lady in Pink is. I haven't been able to visit it since the funeral.

Maria then yelled for Katherine. Seconds later, Katherine rushed into the room and asked, "Is everything okay?"

Maria responded, "Yes, everything is okay. Katherine, can you help me take Marilyn outside?"

"Of course, why outside?" questioned Katherine.

"She asked me to take her to The Lady's grave."

"Okay, let me get on the other side of her. Let's take it easy, Marilyn," said Katherine.

"Katherine, thank you for helping me," softly said Marilyn, struggling to stay balanced.

As they made their way slowly to the tree, Reba followed behind them with a chair for Marilyn to sit in while she visited The Lady in Pink's gravesite. Blossoms began to fall as everyone stood staring in silence at The Lady's gravesite as Marilyn sat. "My…the air is just as fresh as it was when I was a little girl." Marilyn closed her eyes as she felt the breeze blowing through her thinning hair. "If you listen closely, nature has a way of sending messages of love whenever a breeze kisses you on the cheek. It reminds me of The Lady," Marilyn stated as she opened her eyes and stared at The Lady's gravesite. Then, a coo from a dove flying overhead resonated in their heads.

After almost an hour, everyone helped Marilyn back inside the orphanage and Victoria and Caroline prepared dinner. Maria went to the kitchen to help cook and make one of Marilyn's favorite childhood dishes. Meanwhile, Katherine laid alongside Marilyn, holding her hand.

"I love you and can't imagine my life without you. You are my sister to love and fight with," shared Katherine.

Marilyn replied jokingly, "I love you too, Katherine. My life would have been just plain boring without you."

"Let's make each day count. Now I know what The Lady in Pink meant when she said that every day was a gift from God and not to take each other's love for granted," Katherine said while squeezing Marilyn's hand.

As the other women continued preparing dinner, they heard a knock at the door.

"Who could that be?" asked Caroline.

"I don't know," Victoria replied.

"Reba! Answer the door! We are cooking!" Caroline shouted.

"Who's there?" Reba asked, swiftly walking towards the front door.

Reba opened the door, and no one was there.

Suddenly, piercing screams came from Marilyn's room. Everyone immediately rushed into Marilyn's room and found Katherine struggling to calm and restrain Marilyn, who was convulsing and yelling words no one understood. Then, Marilyn abruptly stopped shaking and she said with her eyes closed, *"The Man—So Beautiful… My, Baby!"* Marilyn smiled with a brilliant glow on her face, reached upwards and took her final breath, never completing the sentence.

Tears of a Cherry Blossom Tree

Cries of sorrow and utter shock filled the room and tears streamed down the women's faces. Katherine gripped Marilyn's lifeless hand and seconds later, a white dove landed on the windowsill and cooed loudly. In a rage, Katherine grabbed a bowl that was on the nightstand and threw it at the dove, striking it. The dove cooed after being hit and flew away. "Will someone please hurry and get help? She isn't breathing," Katherine frantically asked, struggling to find her breath and trying to make sense of things.

Victoria answered, "I'll catch a carriage into town and get Dr. Stinson," while running out of the room.

Victoria returned with Dr. Stinson an hour later and he rushed inside with his medicine bag to assess Marilyn. He checked her pulse and heartbeat with a stethoscope and quickly determined that she was gone. He announced to the group, "I'm sorry everyone, but she's no longer with us. There is nothing I can do." Maria, Victoria, Caroline, Reba and Katherine all gathered near Marilyn, wailing in sorrow.

"My sweet Marilyn. No more pain. No more suffering. I will always love you," Maria mourned while holding her hand.

Katherine, wiping away tears, slowly reached inside of Marilyn's dresser drawer for one of her hats. "This is—*was* her favorite pink hat. I'll place it on her head. She will like that." As

Katherine placed the hat on Marilyn's head, the room seemed to sink into deeper sorrow.

"I will go and get Clergyman Madison, so we can prepare the body…I truly am sorry, ladies," Dr. Stinson then hurried out of the room. A few hours later, the doctor returned to the orphanage with Clergyman Madison, who gave his condolences to the women and took Marilyn's body to be prepared for the funeral. Four days later, a memorial service was held by the Cherry Blossom Tree, where Marilyn would be laid to rest next to The Lady in Pink. The remaining four women, Maria and Dr. Stinson attended the service, and Clergyman Madison conducted the eulogy. Towards the end of the service, Clergyman Madison reached down and picked up a few blossoms from the ground and ceremoniously sprinkled them on top of Marilyn's wooden coffin, telling everyone, "You may all come up and pay your respects now." Everyone who attended the funeral one by one said their last goodbyes and placed pink blossoms on top of Marilyn's coffin before heading inside the orphanage. As everyone walked away from the gravesite, they all embraced each other. Katherine, the last to pay her respects, kneeled by her best friend's coffin. She let out a huge sigh and said, "I'm going to miss you, Marilyn. You are my closest friend and sister. I hope you know that you will always be in my heart, and don't worry, I will be here to check on you, okay? *As the moon brightens each midnight sky, so does the sun for each tear I cry.*" Katherine kissed Marilyn's casket for the last time and walked to the orphanage. After she entered the house, Katherine went to remove Marilyn's poetry plate from the cupboard and displayed it next to the picture of The Lady in Pink. Moments later, Maria hugged everyone and made her way back to the North Georgia Mountains.

CHAPTER SIX

THE DIAGNOSIS

*S*everal days later, Katherine and Caroline were in the kitchen making muffins while reminiscing about Marilyn. They all wanted to try to make The Lady in Pink's Cream Cheese Cherry Blossom Muffins after finding her recipe in the kitchen pantry. Then, they heard Caroline scream, "Ow! My legs! My legs are numb! It feels like someone is sticking me with needles! I can barely move them!"

Katherine began cuddling her, frightened by that sudden episode.

"Yikes! It hurts when you touch me!" yelled Caroline, jerking in pain and just as frightened. "What's happening to my legs? I can hardly walk or move!"

"Go and get Dr. Stinson!" shouted Victoria. Katherine and Victoria helped Caroline get into bed. Reba rushed out of the door to get Dr. Stinson.

About an hour later, Dr. Stinson hurried inside the orphanage and raced into Caroline's room with Katherine lying next to her. "What's wrong Caroline?" "My legs are numb. It's quite difficult to move them, doctor. Also, my head is aching and I'm having trouble seeing out of my left eye. What's going on? This has happened before, but no one can tell me what this is!" Caroline wept, afraid and frustrated.

"How long have you been experiencing these symptoms?" Dr. Stinson asked.

"This has been occurring for a little over two years or so and whatever is happening to me seems to be worsening. There are times I go blind in my left eye, get tired easily, fall down, can't walk, and at times feel like needles are sticking me," Caroline explained. Dr. Stinson checked Caroline and reached into his medical bag, pulling out a thick leather covered book. He thumbed through the book for several minutes and then finally stopped on a page. As the doctor started carefully reading the page, he would periodically look up at

Caroline. All of a sudden, Dr. Stinson slammed the leather book close and turned away with his head down.

"What is wrong, Dr. Stinson, could you not find any answers?" Caroline asked nervously.

"I am afraid that these symptoms are related to a rare disease known as Multiple Sclerosis or MS."

Caroline looked around confused, trying to make sense of the diagnosis. "MS?" she said uneasily. Katherine sensed her fear and squeezed her hand in comfort.

"According to the research I have in my book, Dr. Jean-Martin Charcot, a French neurologist, discovered MS in 1868. He found that it is a distinct disease and we know that it attacks the Nervous System, but we are not exactly sure why, or how. Common early signs of this disease are vision problems, numbness, pains and spasms, weakness, cognitive problems, and other symptoms. There are periods of remission and without warning, pain can be crippling. That's why your legs are numb and you're having problems seeing," replied Dr. Stinson.

"Is there a cure for this?" Caroline asked, gripping Katherine's hand, trying to keep her composure.

"I'm afraid not, Caroline."

"I feel like my brain is in a fog. It's hard to think straight. I can't remember things sometimes, is this common with the disease too?" Caroline asked, saddened.

"This is one of the more common symptoms and I would encourage you to get some rest. If I find any treatment that would help, I will let you know. Don't lose faith, Caroline," Dr. Stinson encouraged as he was leaving the room.

Katherine stopped Dr. Stinson as he was exiting the room's door and whispered, "Dr. Stinson, can we talk alone?"

"Of course," Dr. Stinson softly replied.

"How long do we have with her? Days? Months? Years?"

"It's hard to say, but from my assessment, not long. She has most likely had this disease for many years. As a Physician, I don't say this much but I believe prayer is the only remedy for this situation." Katherine placed her hands on her head in anguish and closed her eyes, feeling a complete sense of hopelessness. She then prayed, "God help us, Marilyn and now Caroline. What is going on? What is happening? Maybe—" In the middle of the prayer, Katherine paused, looked at the doctor and said, "I'm sorry Dr. Stinson, I don't mean to hold you with my rambling. Thank you."

The doctor sighed and hugged Katherine. "No need for apologies, please get some rest. You have to take care of yourself also." Katherine nodded and walked Dr. Stinson out the front door. She came back into Caroline's room and sat on the bed next to Caroline, Reba was sitting on the other side of the bed holding Caroline's hand. Victoria was in the kitchen searching for ingredients to make comfort food.

"You know what always makes me feel better? Muffins! I'm going to let Victoria know that Muffins are needed today," said Reba excitedly. She quickly hopped up from Caroline's bed and hurried towards the kitchen. Katherine and Caroline thanked Reba as she left.

"It's alright, Caroline. Just rest up a bit, and your memory will come back. Your parents from New York, do you have their address?" Katherine asked, stroking Caroline's hair.

"Yes, my family," Caroline quietly said, struggling to sit up. "Betty and Jim. Ow, my head hurts very much," she then moaned.

"I hate that you are going through this. How can we contact them?" Katherine hoped Caroline had the ability to remember.

"Um—Oh! The travel route and location are in my purse. They move about quite frequently in New York, conducting fashion shows. It's hard to track down their exact location so it will be better if you traveled there. Here, you can use my train ticket," Caroline replied. Feebly shaking and reaching inside her purse, she handed Katherine a map. "Here is a map marked with some of the common locations they tend to travel to in New York," said Caroline.

Katherine took the travel route, map and train ticket and began packing at once. As she left the room to prepare for the journey, Victoria and Reba were in the kitchen, preparing freshly baked muffins for everyone.

After the muffins were placed in the oven, Reba went back into Caroline's room, to cheer Caroline up with funny stories. Several minutes later, Victoria walked into the room carrying a tray of freshly baked muffins. "I thought that everyone could use some of these," she announced.

"Oh, wow, just like The Lady in Pink made for us. These look so delicious," Caroline smiled as she grabbed a muffin off the tray.

Katherine, who had just entered Caroline's room after packing, took a few muffins, wrapped them up in brown wrapping paper and kissed everyone goodbye.

"Thank you, Katherine. I love you for doing this," said Caroline.

"You're welcome. I know you would do the same for me. I will be back with your family," promised Katherine before walking out of the door carrying her bags.

"Safe travels and we love you!" shouted Reba and Victoria after her.

"Be careful," whispered Caroline. The town's carriage driver, Kobe Alexander, arrived just in time as he was passing through the town of Macon for travelers needing a ride.

Katherine waved and shouted, "Greetings, Kobe!"

He stopped the carriage and tilted his top hat in respect. "Greetings, Miss Katherine, you are looking quite lovely this fine afternoon. I've had such an interesting day with my Aunt Rosie and Uncle Cleotus! Let me tell you, those two are quite the pair! I love them, but they are a pain in my side at times! They love snooping around, I caught them wondering around the stables this morning for God knows what. They're not the brightest tool in the shed, but they're hilarious and seem to just show up out of nowhere! But Georgia Boy here stopped their snooping escapade, didn't you, Boy?" Kobe proudly looked at his horse, Georgia Boy, and then continued, "He ran them clean out of the stables!" Kobe let out a laugh and resumed, "I won't see them snooping around my place any time soon!" chuckled Kobe. Then, he looked down at Katherine, who was waiting patiently for him to finish his story. Kobe quickly apologized,

"Oh, how rude of me! Let me help you climb aboard! I'll take your suitcase."

"Thank you, Kobe. And yes, Cleotus and Rosey are quite the troublesome pair," laughed Katherine.

"Where to, Miss Katherine?" asked Kobe.

"I am headed to the train station to make my way to New York," replied Katherine.

"As you wish," kindly replied Kobe. Off they went, heading to the train station.

Katherine mistakenly left the front door of the orphanage ajar and a dove flew inside. The dove fluttered throughout the rooms before coming to rest at the foot of Caroline's bed.

"Oh my, look how beautiful! Her wings look like the wings of an angel!" remarked Caroline, smiling and staring at the dove. "Please, please, let her stay with me for a little while. Doves are peaceful to look at," she pleaded to Reba and Victoria.

The dove cooed while spreading its wings.

Reba, Victoria and Caroline stared in amazement while quietly holding each other, trying not to scare away the dove. The dove cooed seven times in a row and seemed to be staring directly at Caroline.

"Why did the dove coo seven times? What could that mean?" Reba questioned.

"Maybe it's a sign or something," said Victoria, puzzled.

"Maybe it's talking to us. Could it be a sign that I will be going to heaven soon?" sniffed Caroline.

"Could the dove represent an angel? Also, how do you know if it's a male or female dove? Whatever it is, it's quite beautiful. Wait… is that the same dove that was here when Marilyn died or is it another dove?" rambled Victoria.

Reba started to get irritated after hearing the conversations and shouted, "Enough about the bird, you two! Let's not talk about this anymore. We've dealt with too much death as it is. Let's just turn in for the night."

"What about the dove?" asked Caroline.

"I will open the door and shoo it outside," snapped Reba.

"No, please don't. I want it to stay with me," said Caroline.

"Okay, okay. We will close your door and leave the dove inside your room for the night, isn't that right, Reba?" said Victoria while firmly staring at Reba, demanding that she comply.

Reba sighed in defeat and agreed with Victoria, "I suppose we can release it in the morning."

"Thank you both, I keep hearing a song in my head and the words are *We shall behold Him*. I can't remember how I know the song, but it's beautiful." She began softly humming to the song in her head and slowly started drifting off to sleep.

Reba left the room slowly without frightening the dove and closed the front door that Katherine accidentally left open earlier before returning to Caroline's room. However, she didn't realize that the window was slightly open in Caroline's room. She eased slowly back inside the room where Caroline had finally fallen asleep. Reba then cautiously climbed into bed with Victoria and Caroline. The dove on the footboard didn't move or flinch at all. It was stiff as a statue, staring at Caroline with such an intensity. Tired from the day, Reba and Victoria quickly dozed off to sleep.

The next morning, Caroline woke up and noticed that the dove was no longer at the foot of the bed. "Reba! Reba! Wake up! It's gone! It's gone! You must go and find her! Please!" shouted Caroline.

Reba was startled awake by all the shouting and embraced Caroline to calm her. "It's alright. I'll go find the dove. I'm sure it's somewhere in the house," said Reba. She got out of bed calling for the dove, looking in each room, and then returned to Caroline's room. When Reba returned to Caroline's room, she noticed the window was slightly open and a feather was on the windowsill. Reba realized that the dove left through the open window in her room. *"God, how am I going to break the news to Caroline? She's going to be so sad. Help me please,"* prayed Reba.

She walked slowly over to Caroline and sat alongside her bed, holding her hand. Hesitating to break the news, Reba reached over and grabbed Caroline's other hand. Victoria overheard the conversation as she awakened. "Caroline, sometimes the hardest thing in life is letting go of the things. The dove, unfortunately, is gone, but I'm sure it will come back to you one day," Reba tenderly said. Caroline pulled Reba and Victoria closer while embracing them. "Thank you both," said Caroline.

Almost three weeks had passed by and Caroline, although still sick, didn't seem to be getting worse. One afternoon, she decided to sneak out of bed and into the kitchen to prepare sandwiches. She made the sandwiches not only for herself but also for Reba and Victoria, who were both outside washing linens and hanging them to dry. After Caroline finished making the sandwiches, she quietly grabbed one and started to tip-toe back to her room. Just then,

Victoria and Reba walked back inside and caught Caroline trying to sneak back to her room. "Caroline!" yelled Victoria, frowning with hands on her hips. "What are you doing out of bed?" she finished. "Do you need to be restrained?" questioned Reba, in a stern tone. Caroline looked at both of them with a guilty, child-like look on her face and replied, "I made you sandwiches too." Reba and Victoria looked at each other and laughed at Caroline's response and expression. Reba then walked over to Caroline and helped her back to the room and Victoria grabbed the sandwiches from the kitchen and brought them to Caroline's room.

As they began eating, someone knocked at the door. "Maybe it's Dr. Stinson coming back to check on you," said Reba, hurrying towards the front door. It was Katherine at the door with Caroline's family from New York.

"Katherine! You made it back! It's been a while. Caroline! it's Katherine! She found your family! Please come in, everyone. She's back here," said Reba, excitedly.

They all followed Reba into Caroline's bedroom and gasped. They found Caroline lying on the floor crying with Victoria sitting on the floor beside her, rocking and consoling her.

"Caroline! Were you trying to get up?" asked Reba, concerned.

Caroline nodded, still crying. Caroline's adoptive father, Jim, ran to pick her up and then gently placed her back in bed. Jim and Betty embraced Caroline and assessed her to see if she had hurt herself from the fall.

"Dear, you scared us half to death," Betty said in relief after they confirmed Caroline was not injured, then she said choking back tears, "We love you so much and left New York as soon as Katherine arrived. Know that we are going to be by your side, through it all."

"We will fight with you and for you," Jim said with a half-smile and holding her hand. Katherine walked into the room and gave everyone a glass of sweetened tea.

"This is quite refreshing, Katherine. Thank you so much. For everything. This is just what I needed after such a long trip," Jim said.

"You're welcome. No one makes tea like the south, Mr. Jim."

"This is quite delicious, Katherine," complimented Betty.

Reba then treated everyone to a bowl of soup and sandwiches.

Several days passed by with laughter, memories, and joys of her childhood in New York. One fateful day, Caroline began experiencing high fevers that wouldn't go away, severe pain of her upper and lower extremity, paralysis, and shortness of breath.

"Caroline, please be okay. You mean the world to us. Please don't leave us. We just wish the pain would go away," Betty cried.

"Jim, will you please read your favorite bible passage that you used to read to me when I was little?" asked Caroline.

"Sure, Sweetheart," Jim replied tearfully as he pulled out his bible and read a passage from Psalms 91.

"Thank you. I dreamt last night of the most beautiful place I'd ever seen. I saw The Lady in Pink, Marilyn, and a Man in White. Oh, and believe it or not—flying creatures. They were all waiting on the other side of a river. I heard them call my name and say it was time for me to come home. I felt no pain at all. I could see and walk, and my memory was clear. Mother, Father, I want you to know that I love you so much and thanks for always standing by me… Please call my dear sisters inside," she requested.

"Of course," Betty sobbed. "Katherine! Reba! Victoria! Caroline is asking for you all."

"We're on our way," responded Katherine as the other women followed her inside the room.

"Can we recite our childhood poetry again?" asked Caroline weakly.

"We would love to," Reba said in tears.

Reba started reciting her plate's poem, *"With happiness and cheers, I can chase away my fears."*

Victoria's lips quivered as she said, *"Let peace be still to one and all, no matter how great, no matter how small."*

Katherine closed her eyes and softly spoke, *"As the moon brightens each midnight sky, so does the sun for each tear I cry."*

Caroline asked for help, as she had forgotten the lines of her poetry plate. The former orphans all grabbed each other's hands and in unison cited Caroline's poem aloud, *"No matter how heavy my heart may be, I can always find love underneath the Cherry Blossom Tree."* Caroline suddenly passed out but was still breathing.

The familiar dove unexpectedly flew into the room, landing at the foot of her bed, cooing loudly. "No, get away you evil bird! Something always happens whenever you come here!" yelled Katherine with fury.

"It looks as if it's staring right at Caroline," said Jim, looking on with surprise. Katherine chased the dove out of the open bedroom window.

Hours passed into the early morning. Betty lied alongside Caroline, cuddling her while Jim slept in the chair.

"Good morning, Caroline," said Betty as she awakened, but Caroline didn't respond. "Good morning, Caroline," repeated Betty louder and worried, simultaneously shaking Jim awake.

Seeing the fear on his wife's face, Jim rushed over to Caroline's bed and shook her while yelling at her to wake up. Panicking, he quickly pressed his fingers against her neck to check for a pulse and held his ear close to her mouth to see if she's breathing.

"Caroline! Caroline, Honey! Wake Up! Oh! No! Help us! She's not breathing! She's not breathing!" shouted Jim in disbelief.

Betty crumbled to the floor, crying hysterically. Reba, Victoria, and Katherine all came running into the room. "What's wrong? Oh! No!" they shouted, as they look over at Caroline's still body.

Katherine began weeping uncontrollably as Betty laid rocking on the floor in grief. Jim began crying inconsolably while holding Caroline's lifeless body in his arms.

"Caroline! Caroline! Wake up! Not you too!" Katherine cried.

"Please wake up Caroline! We need you!" Reba said stone-faced.

"No. This can't be. I thought she had longer!" Victoria said hysterically.

Caroline still didn't respond. Reba ran out of the house to get Dr. Stinson while everyone in the house tried to console one another.

A short time later, Dr. Stinson ran straight to Caroline's room. He checked several times for a pulse and breathing. "She's gone, everyone. I knew this disease was aggressive, but I was hoping she had more time," confirmed Dr. Stinson.

After the confirmation everyone gathered around Caroline's bedside, each of them kissing her on the cheek before saying goodbye. Suddenly, Caroline opened her eyes wide and bolted upright in the bed. Everyone jumped back, and Betty fainted immediately.

"Uh—Uh—Run and get the smelling salts!" yelled Jim incredulously, backing away slowly from the bed with wide-eyes.

"She's back! She's back! It's a miracle!" stammered Victoria.

Caroline coughed twice and stared unblinkingly. She then stated in a faraway voice, "I came back to tell you all not to worry about me. I am in a much better place, just as I dreamed. I no longer feel any pain. I saw *His* face. *His* beautiful eyes. They are filled with so much love. I love you all. I see angels coming for…" Caroline stopped and stared at Katherine.

Then, with a glowing, luminous smile on her face, Caroline let out a long, steady breath before closing her eyes and falling back limp on the bed.

"She's gone again! Please come back!" cried Katherine holding Caroline's limp hand.

Dr. Stinson, in a state of shock and disbelief, straightened his glasses on his face and rushed over to take a final check of Caroline's pulse. "How could this happen? This defies any medical explanation! She was not breathing and had no pulse!" Noticeably shaking and looking at his pocket watch, Dr. Stinson called Caroline's time of death for the second time that day. Dr. Stinson then made a quick exit from the room without glancing back.

Days Later, Caroline's memorial was held under The Cherry Blossom Tree. The remaining three orphans all held hands before the funeral service began and made a tribute to Caroline by singing *"Up and down we go, her pain will be no more, skip around the Cherry Blossom Tree, now rest forever more."* The tree seemed to shed tears of Cherry Blossoms as the mysterious dove comes to rest in the treetops.

Victoria looked at the dove in the treetops and began singing the song that Caroline used to enjoy, *We Shall Behold Him*. Reba, Catherine, Jim, Betty, and Dr. Stinson joined Victoria in singing, and a warm breeze came through the tree branches as they all sung together.

Clergyman Madison officiated the service by starting out with Caroline's favorite poetry, *"No matter how heavy my heart may be, I can always find love underneath the Cherry Blossom Tree."* Then, he opened his King James Bible and read, *"Revelations 21:4 tells us that God shall wipe away all tears from their eyes; and there shall be no more death, neither sorrow, nor crying, neither shall there be any more pain: for the former things are passed away."* He picked up Cherry Blossoms and began speaking about their beauty. "We all miss her dearly, but she's in a far better place as she told us. Let's remember Caroline by celebrating her life with continued love for each other. May she forever rest in peace and enjoy her eternal home of love," lovingly said Clergyman Madison.

Everyone picked up blossoms and sprinkled them on the coffin as it was lowered into the grave. On her tombstone, her favorite lines of poetry were engraved, *"No matter how heavy my heart may be, I can always find love underneath the Cherry Blossom Tree."*

A Sinking Feeling

They all walked away with their heads down and cried with heavy hearts. As the saddened group walked back to the orphanage, three large branches snapped off The Cherry Blossom Tree and they all looked back at it, "It's like the Tree is dying now too. Everything seems to be dying around here," said Victoria.

On the way back to the orphanage, Jim nearly fainted in despair and grief. Betty, Clergy Madison, Dr. Stinson, and all the other women rushed to his side to steady him. After Dr. Stinson attended to him, Jim smiled to assure everyone that he was okay. He resumed slowly walking toward the front door of the orphanage, with the aid of Dr. Stinson and Clergy Madison. Once inside, Betty led Jim to rest in one of the empty rooms.

Katherine and Victoria helped Reba to her room after she proclaimed to them, "I'm feeling tired. I simply can't handle any more funerals."

"I'll get you some water and a cool wet towel. We all have been through too much," Katherine replied. Katherine left and came back with a cold wet towel, which she applied to Reba's forehead while giving her water. Reba finally calmed down, but she was pale white and breathing abnormally. "I will be back in a moment, Reba," Katherine left to talk to Victoria.

Tears of a Cherry Blossom Tree

"Victoria, can you come to my room, please? I need to speak with you for a moment,"

"Of course, Katherine," Victoria entered Katherine's room. Katherine was fidgety, pacing back and forth in her room. "Close the door behind you, please."

"What's wrong Katherine?"

"Can't you see? Everything is wrong. First, The Lady in Pink, then Marilyn and Caroline, now Reba isn't looking very good. What is going on here? Do you think we're under some sort of curse?" Katherine whispered in a frantic voice.

"You're scaring me, Katherine. I mean, to be honest, the same kind of thought crossed my mind, but I don't believe in curses. Besides, we are good people, we love, we care, we live honest lives, and we're certainly not bootleggers. We pray and do decent things. Why on earth would we be cursed?" Victoria questioned, pondering the thought.

They both sat on Katherine's bed as she let out a sigh. "I don't know what to do. What if I'm right? Should we leave this house and go far away?" Katherine sighed and reflected for a few seconds. "Oh, maybe you're right. I suppose I'm going mad."

"I'm always right, and you've always been quite mad," Victoria grinned, shoulder bumping Katherine.

"Alright, let's go check on Reba. If she looks worse, I'll head into town and send a telegram to her family, just so they are aware of her condition. Maybe they'll have answers as to why she is this way," hoped Katherine.

"Okay. Everything will be alright, just have faith," responded Victoria. Katherine smiled, and they both embraced one another before leaving the room.

Katherine went back to Reba's bed and saw her faint appearance, "Reba, I would like to get in contact with your family. I can go into town to send them a telegram, if you like. I remember them from when we met at the Olympic championships in France," Katherine said.

Reba, pale and starting to sweat profusely, looked at Katherine and said, "Katherine, grab my purse, please," Katherine picked up Reba's purse from the floor and handed it to her. "I'm sure I'll be fine, so don't scare them," instructed Reba as she dug in her purse and pulled out a piece of paper and some money. "Here's their current address in Switzerland, they move there because of the war scare. Here, please take some extra money." Katherine took the address and money from Reba and then headed out the door to go into town.

Throughout the next several days, Katherine, Betty and Victoria continued to tend Reba; her condition was not showing much sign of improvement. Victoria prepared breakfast and lunch and Betty prepared dinner while Katherine constantly watched over Reba. Reba always pitched in whenever she felt better, but she knew something unusual was happening to her.

Meanwhile, Jim continued to grieve over the loss of Caroline. He struggled to eat and cried daily underneath the Cherry Blossom Tree, where Caroline's grave was. He would sometimes remain there until dark and had to be called inside. Betty and Victoria did everything possible to help him get through the depression. Finally, they sent for Dr. Stinson after noticing Jim was not responding to simple commands. Upon Dr. Stinson's arrival, he walked over to Jim, who was outside sitting with his back against the tree. "Jim, how are you? It's me again, Dr. Stinson."

Jim was unresponsive and emotionless as he stared at the sketched picture of Caroline he found in her room.

"Jim? How—"

Jim interrupted the doctor, blurting out, "How am I? *Jeez*, Doc. How! Am! I? You're useless."

The doctor took a slow step back, staring at Jim sideways, "I don't understand Jim, what do you mean?"

Jim continued, "You heard me, Doc, You…Are…Useless, why are you even here? All of your so-called knowledge, books, and abilities are just plain useless, can't you see? We all… are just… plain useless," expressed Jim in a delirious, somber tone. "I couldn't keep my beautiful Caroline alive and neither could you, Doc. This is your fault, you're supposed to heal and fix people, but you deliver nothing except news of death. You're nothing more than a grim reaper— Yeah…that's what you are, Doc—Just a grim reaper pretending to be a doctor. If you haven't figured it out by now, this family is cursed, The Lady in Pink, the Marilyn girl, my Caroline! Look at Reba; she may very well be the next victim of this *curse*! God, if there is one, took my precious Caroline. For what? Why, Doc? Why didn't the *Almighty God* just take me, why didn't he just take me instead?" Jim yelled in defeat and gloom while staring up into the cloudy, bright sky with hopelessness.

Dr. Stinson walked over closer to Jim, kneeled down by his side, and said, "Jim, listen, I wish I had an answer for all of this, but I don't. I wish that I could help every single soul I encounter, but I can't. All of my knowledge and skills simply can't fix death. But I always have hope, and I can always provide comfort. Everyone questions God and his plans at times, even the existence of God, but you know, it helps when I just trust that everything has a purpose. It makes me feel better. I just do the best with what I have, and I find peace in that alone. Jim, I'm deeply sorry about Caroline, but I believe you are still here for a reason and it's up to you and you alone to find that reason."

Jim said nothing, as he was sitting down with his head and back against the tree, staring upwards.

"I'm here if you need me, Jim," said Dr. Stinson in a worried tone. The doctor got up and went into the orphanage to talk to Betty.

"Betty, I'm afraid Jim's depression and grief are quite severe. Please give him this medicine every four hours. It will help him sleep."

"Thank you, Dr. Stinson." Betty followed the doctor's instructions by giving Jim the medication while he was outside. An hour later, Jim finally came inside the house to sleep for the first time in days.

Betty began telling Victoria stories about Jim and Caroline when they first picked her up from Stillwaters. "Jim and Caroline had a special father and daughter bond. "I can remember on the ship the journey back home after picking her up. Caroline Saxon was only seven years old with such beautiful, brunette hair and green eyes. She was the prettiest little girl and she loved Jim like a father. I had never seen him so happy. On board the ship, Jim and Caroline danced to classical music and the bystanders cheered and applauded the performance. They were marvelous together." Betty patted her eyes with a handkerchief and continued her story. "Honestly, I believe modeling was always in her genes from the way she pranced her way back to her seat after the dance. Once we arrived home, she and Jim would dance to classical music after she completed her homework. Those were priceless moments and I don't know if Jim is ever going to get over her loss. I have never seen him like this. It's as if he has nothing else to live for," Betty said with tears flowing down her cheeks.

"Have you or Jim been able to go into Caroline's room?" Victoria asked.

"Oh, heavens no, dear. It would bring back so many memories of Caroline. I don't believe any of us could handle it. We just have to find a way to cope with her being gone. They both remained silent for a moment. "Oh, by the way, how is Reba feeling?" asked Betty, changing the subject.

"I'm about to go check on her now actually, you can come with me if you would like, Mrs. Betty. It's been about an hour since I've last seen her. Katherine is still resting in her room after staying up all of last night with Reba," said Victoria. They both got up to check on Reba and found her sleeping soundly. Victoria walked closer to Reba's side and whispered to Betty, "It's good to see that she's finally getting some rest now."

"Indeed, it is. Katherine mentioned earlier that she will take the night shift to watch Reba," replied Betty in a whisper.

"I'm getting tired now. I will see you in the morning. Good night, Mrs. Betty,"

"Good night, Victoria."

A week later, there was a knock at the door. Katherine looked outside and opened the door with a greeting. "Welcome, everyone. I wasn't sure if you were coming," said Katherine.

At the door was Reba's adoptive father, Nathan, adoptive mother, Camila and adoptive brother, Ethan. "I am so glad you all made it.

"Yes, it was so thoughtful of you to send the telegram. Otherwise, we wouldn't have known. As soon as we got the message, we decided to leave and come see about her right away. We tried to contact her husband Alexandre in France, but we never received a message back. There is a war heading that way and we all pray that he is safe. It's good to see you all again. The last time we met was at the World Figure Skating Championship," said Camila.

Katherine recalled the sight of watching Reba figure skate. "We can never forget those wonderful moments. She was so graceful as a figure skater. I've never seen such a beautiful spectacle of twirls, jumps and dancing on ice. I remember her last jump, it seemed like she spun around fifty times while in the air. It was marvelous! Oh, there I go again babbling about, she's this way." Katherine led the family to Reba's room and when they entered the doorway Katherine announced, "Reba, I have some visitors for you."

"Oh! Nathan, Camila, Ethan, I am so glad you're here," Reba said excitedly.

"Why, we've traveled with you all these years while you were skating. Why stop now?" Nathan asked, chuckling. He then walked over to Reba and kissed her on the forehead.

"You all look so wonderful and I've sorely missed you all so much," said Reba.

"You look wonderful and we've missed you as well, dear" replied Camila as she walked over to kiss and hug Reba.

"Ethan, big brother, come over here. You're so handsome. That slick black hair with that square jaw must have every woman in France chasing you. You definitely got your handsome looks from me," joked Reba.

Ethan laughed and went over and gave Reba a hug and kiss on the cheek, "Thank you for the compliment but all I care about is having my ice-skating partner back." Ethan then stared at Reba with a serious look and tapped his finger on his chin as though he was pondering a thought. He then said, "I know what the problem is Reba! You're probably not feeling well because you need the ice rink, like a fish needs water," joked Ethan with a big smile.

Everyone in the room laughed. Reba sat up and said to her adoptive family, "This means the world to me. there's nothing like having family and friends beside you during these times, Nathan, I have never forgotten the moment you arrived to pick me up from Stillwaters as a child. Sailing home, I remember feeding seagulls, eating candies and instantly knowing that you were my father. I love you so much," Reba said, holding Nathan's hand.

"Camila, I will never forget the words you used when I stepped inside your home, calling me your daughter. I really felt like it was my home and you made me feel welcomed. I love you," Reba said, holding her hand.

"I love you more, Reba," replied Camila.

"And Ethan. You told me that you were glad that I arrived and that you always wanted a sister. I hope that I have lived up to your expectations because you have exceeded mine. You were the reason I became an Olympic figure skater and won those medals. You taught me how to skate and I never wanted to let my brother down. I love you," Reba said, smiling.

"I couldn't have asked for a better sister than you. I've missed you and the times we spent skating. I was always proud of you as my sister more so than a skater," Ethan said.

"Katherine, thank you so much for reaching out to them."

"You're welcome and that's what I am here for," replied Katherine with a wink.

"Nathan—Where is Alexandre?" asked Reba, sounding concerned and slightly disappointed.

Nathan sat on Reba's bed and was quiet for a few seconds and said, "I don't know, dear. We sent him a telegram and never got a message back."

Reba tried to think of why Alexandre didn't respond. She eventually reasoned, "Maybe it be something with the War? Before I left, he mentioned that the military needed his aid to provide prosthetics for wounded soldiers. I hope he is okay."

"I'm sure he is fine, Reba. Things are quite chaotic in France. I heard from a friend in France that communication stations have prioritized transmissions more for the war efforts. The surrounding countries need all the help they get."

"I see... I pray he's alright," hoped Reba.

As breakfast was being prepared by Victoria, everyone could smell the biscuits, eggs, bacon and coffee aroma.

"Something smells good," Nathan said.

"This is what you call a Southern breakfast served with Southern hospitality," Katherine laughed.

"I can't wait to eat, I'll help you get out of bed first, Reba," Ethan said as he moved in to assist Reba out of Bed.

"Thank you, Ethan," smiled Reba.

"Why don't I show you all to your room? You sure you don't need help, Ethan?" Victoria asked. Ethan smiled and shook his head saying no, gradually helping Reba get out of the bed.

"Sure, we will follow you," Camila replied.

Moments later, everyone including Jim and Betty joined Victoria for breakfast. Katherine took Caroline's poetry plate out of the cupboard. She placed it alongside Marilyn's poetry plate. "There are only three more remaining in the cupboard," sighed Katherine. While everyone was at the table preparing to eat, Reba began holding her stomach and moaning in agony. When she tried to stand up to leave the kitchen table, she moaned even louder. Katherine swiftly grabbed Reba by her arm to support her and escorted her back to her room and into bed. Nathan, Camila and Ethan all left the table to follow Reba to her room. They all gathered around her bedside holding her hands and consoling her.

Jim and Betty came into Reba's room after everyone else. "Are you okay?" Jim asked. That was the first time he had said a word to anyone that day.

"No, I can hardly breathe," wailed Reba.

Katherine then said, "Let me have Dr. Stinson come and check on you. Please stay close until I return."

"We will," Camila said while holding Reba's hand.

Katherine rushed into town and managed to catch Dr. Stinson just as he was about to leave his office. "Dr. Stinson, you must come and check on Reba. She's very ill," Katherine pleaded to the doctor.

"I'll grab my things. You can ride back with me in my carriage," he said. After the doctor grabbed his medical bag from the office, they raced back to the orphanage.

CHAPTER SEVEN

THE MANIFESTATION

*U*pon arrival, Dr. Stinson made his way to Reba's room. "How are you doing, Reba?" he asked.

"Not good at all. I'm getting worse by the minute seems like," she moaned.

"Here, let me check," said Dr. Stinson. While checking her breathing, he noticed Reba's short, raspy breaths. "I can tell you're struggling to breathe. I can hear your speech slurring as you talk, also. Can you get up and walk for me?" he questioned.

"No, my legs are too weak."

"Let me help you," said Dr. Stinson.

"Could it be that she has the same problem as Caroline?" asked Jim. Betty was startled to see her husband so alert and talkative.

"I'm not sure until I conduct some more tests," he replied to Jim. "Follow my finger with your eyes. Inhale and exhale for me. Ok, now, hold on to me as you try to stand up," Dr. Stinson reached out to support Reba.

"Ow! My legs are hurting. Please let me lie down," begged Reba.

Dr. Stinson eased Reba back down on to the bed and helped tuck her in.

"What is it? What's wrong with me? I can hardly hold my head up," she fearfully stated.

Dr. Stinson immediately grabbed a thick, leather book out of his medical bag and opened it. He began to flip and scroll down numerous pages. A few moments later, he stopped on a page and read it intensely. He then placed the book on the corner of the bed, took off his glasses and looked at Reba. The doctor took in a deep breath and slowly released it. "All of the signs and symptoms that you are having, lead me to believe that you have ALS, Reba…Known as Amyotrophic Lateral Sclerosis. The first symptoms are muscle twitching and weakness in a limb, or slurred speech. Eventually, it affects the muscles needed to move, speak, eat, and breathe. And currently, there is no cure for ALS," explained Dr. Stinson, placing his hand on top of Reba's.

"So, there isn't anything we can do to help her?" asked Katherine, searching for a glimpse of hope.

"Honestly, there's not much you can do. Just make her as comfortable as you can. I'm afraid this kind of disease advances rapidly," affirmed the doctor with sympathy.

Jim folded his arm and started pacing back and forth in the room, "What's the story behind this illness, Doc?"

Dr. Stinson opened his book again and thumbed through the pages again, "Hmm…Oh, here it is. Well, Jim, it tells me that Dr. Jean-Martin Charcot, the same person who discovered Caroline's disease, Multiple Sclerosis, also founded the disease ALS or amyotrophic lateral sclerosis. It is a progressive neurodegenerative disease that affects nerve cells in the brain and the spinal cord. This causes the loss of function of the body and eventually paralyzes. That's all we know about the disease today."

"I couldn't save my own daughter, at least let me help you with her. By the way, Doc, I'm sorry for what I said to you the last time we talked. I know you were trying to help," Jim said, fighting back tears and still pacing about.

"Please don't apologize, Jim, I completely understand that you were hurting and I'm still here for you and this family, whenever you all need me," assured Dr. Stinson.

Camila and Nathan, aware of Jim's grief, hugged and consoled him. "We're here for you and pray for you each night. We thank you for caring about our daughter. We all appreciate you for standing by her and us," Nathan said.

"It all just hurts so badly. I can't believe my little girl is gone. We can get through this, right?" Jim sobbed.

"Of course, Jim. We got each other," Camila said in tears.

"Come over here and sit next to me, Jim. I miss Caroline just as much as you do, but she would want you to be strong. I need you to be strong for me. I am so very grateful that you are here with me," Reba said with a smile.

"I'm here for you, Reba. Whatever you need, I'm here," Jim sobbed as he hugged Reba. He then dried his eyes and got up, telling everyone goodnight before heading to his room.

Katherine followed Jim into his room and sat alongside him on the bed. She put her hand on his back and said to him, "You are going to be alright. Please don't give up. We're here for you, I hope you know that."

He turned and looked at Katherine with watery eyes, "Thank you for being here through all of this and comforting all of us, you have such a strong and kind spirit. You remind so much of The Lady in Pink."

"That's quite flattering, but The Lady in Pink was a much better person than me," Katherine chuckled a bit and sighed, "I wish she was still here. Life seemed so easy, joyous and safe whenever she was around," Katherine then got up from the bed, looked at Jim with a smile and said, "Try to get some rest." Katherine left him to rest and closed the door.

While in the hallway, she started talking to herself. "Why are these horrible things happening to us? The Lady in Pink, Marilyn, Caroline and now Reba. What did we do to deserve this? It has to be something with this place, a plague, the Tree—or that Evil Dove! That's what it is The Dove! If I ever see it around here again, I'm going to…" Katherine took in a deep breath and slowly let it out to calm herself. She then silently cried to herself, "None of this makes sense."

As nightfall approached, everyone decided to turn in to bed early and Katherine slept alongside Reba for the night.

Late into the night, Reba was awakened by the sound of fluttering wings as a mysterious dove hovered over her head. "You're are so beautiful. Am I dreaming?" whispered Reba, smiling at the dove.

At the sound of the coo, Katherine jumped out of bed startled, "Get out of here and don't come back!" she screamed. "That dove is bad news. It's Evil! *Cursed*!" Katherine wildly shooed the dove away and it flew back out through the open window. A ray of glistening, white light followed the dove as it disappeared into the night sky.

"Hmm, did you see that, Reba?"

"Yes, it was the most beautiful sight that I have ever seen," Responded Reba, wide-eyed. "You know—I think I'm getting better. I still feel pain but is not as bad anymore. Maybe it's a miracle! God, please let it be a miracle. Um, maybe if I lay down and get more rest, it will speed up the miracle, what do you think Katherine?" Reba asked.

Katherine got back in the bed with Reba and stared up at the ceiling and softly replied, "Anything is possible, Reba."

Reba smiled and leaned over to kissed Katherine on the cheek, before turning over to go to sleep. Katherine looked over at Reba with a soft smiled, eventually dozing off to sleep.

When dawn arrived, the orphanage filled with the aroma of biscuits, bacon and eggs. Camila and Victoria were in the kitchen preparing breakfast for everyone.

"I think we should take the poetry plates down before Reba awakes," proposed Victoria.

"That's a great idea. She will like that," Katherine agreed.

Victoria started placing the poetry plates on the kitchen table. "The smell of bacon and breakfast brings back memories of our wonderful time here with The Lady in Pink. It is astounding how we became one big happy family in such a short time. We loved playing underneath the Cherry Blossom Tree and skipping around it while singing," reminisced Victoria.

Victoria and Katherine slowly looked at each other with a grin and began singing, "*Up and down we go, now hop and touch your toes, skip around the Cherry Blossom Tree, now stop and touch your nose,*" Reba joined in the song from her bedroom.

"Reba's awake! Let's go check on her," said Katherine.

"I will stay here and make sure nothing burns. Why don't you go?" insisted Victoria.

Katherine left the kitchen and eased into Reba's bedroom.

"Good morning. Victoria and Camila are making your favorite breakfast. Were you singing along with us?" asked Katherine.

"Yes, it brought back memories. I had a dream about her last night that The Lady was calling my name," said Reba.

"What else did she say?" asked Katherine.

"She just smiled and stretched out her arms and faded away."

"Breakfast is ready everyone!" Victoria shouted.

Katherine went into the kitchen to prepare Reba's breakfast plate. Soon after, Jim, Betty and Reba's adoptive family piled into the kitchen. Victoria served plates for everyone and Camila carried several glasses of milk on a tray to Reba's room. Everyone in the house went into Reba's bedroom to keep Reba company. "Compliments of Victoria and Camila. Thank you all," said Reba with watery eyes.

"Let's bless our meal. Lord, thank you for this meal and all the hands that prepared it. Even though I have a hard time swallowing it, I ask that you allow me to enjoy the love of the family and friends that surround me. Amen," prayed Reba.

Everyone sat on the floor, along the bed and in chairs joining Reba for breakfast. They all laughed, told stories and enjoyed the precious moment with one another.

There was a loud knock at the door and Nathan went to answer it. "Who's there?"

No one answered the first time. Nathan pulled back the curtain and noticed a face pressed against the windowpane with crossed-eyes. "Ah! Who are you?" asked Nathan, startled.

"It's ya friendly neighbor down the street. Some call me Cleotus but you can't believe ever thang ya hear. This here is my wife, Rosey. Smile for him, darling. She's one of a kind. It sometimes makes me jealous. What's ya name fuzzball?" Cleotus asked.

"Hold on a minute," Nathan said stone-faced closing the curtains. He walked back to Reba's room with a confused look on his face.

"Do any of you know of a strange couple by the names of Cleotus and Rosey?" asked Nathan.

Reba, Victoria and Katherine all laughed. "Oh dear, yes, we know them quite well. I'm pretty sure everyone in Macon, Georgia has heard of them. They are our neighbors, Nathan," Katherine said with a light-hearted laugh.

"Please send them back to my room," said Reba.

Katherine went back to the door and opened it. "Please come in."

Cleotus and Rosey stepped inside and immediately headed for the stove where the leftover biscuits and bacon were. "My, I remember y'all as young'uns. I know y'all miss The Lady," Cleotus said.

"Yes, we do," Katherine replied.

"Cleotus! Come here for a moment," Reba said.

"Did I hear someone call for Cleotus?" he asked.

"Yes, I believe it was Reba, follow me this way," instructed Katherine.

"It's so good to see you two. Have a seat," Reba said.

"Don't mind if I do," said Cleotus.

"Sweetie, why are you in this bed?" asked Rosey.

"Well, I am not feeling well and just need some rest," answered Reba. "I haven't seen you all since The Lady's memorial service, and just wanted to say thank you for being such good neighbors to her."

"She was a special lady and you all brought her so much joy," Rosey said.

"She sure did, I think of her all of the time. So, Rosey, Katherine told me about the time Cleotus ran down the street with holes in the back of his pants grabbing his trousers while eating hot chicken. Is any of that true?" Reba laughed, snorting a bit.

Cleotus and Rosey began laughing along with Reba and everyone in the room.

Katherine introduced everyone to Cleotus and Rosey. "What brings you two here today? No, don't tell me. Was it the...?" Reba started to finish the sentence and then paused.

"Yes, it was the biscuits and bacon we smelled coming down the road," Rosey confessed while laughing.

"Ew, what kinda cologne are you wearing Cleotus?" asked Reba.

"My favorite! Skunk Supreme," answered Cleotus with a laugh.

Everyone laughed, and spirits seemed to come alive. "Thank you all for making my day," Reba said.

"Take care of yourself, Reba," Rosey said, hugging her.

"Come here, Cleotus, you can hug me too," Reba said smiling. "Take care and don't forget to grab some breakfast on the way out."

"Of course not lil' sickly gurl, why you think we came in the first place!" laughed Cleotus. "Anywho, God bless ya and all that other stuff," Cleotus continued as he was leaving out of Reba's room with

biscuit crumbs falling out of his back pockets and bacon grease stains that could be seen on the back of his trousers. Everyone laughed, and Katherine provided them both with a hearty breakfast before they headed back home.

CHAPTER EIGHT

THE STANDOFF

Days following, Reba became weaker and in need of more care. Katherine and Camila were constantly by her side while Betty and Victoria prepared meals.

Reba started coughing uncontrollably. It looked like she wanted to speak. She kept pointing to her throat, but she only managed to get out a garbled, "Can't... swallow."

Dr. Stinson arrived for his daily check and confirmed that Reba's symptoms were worsening.

"I'm tired. I am going back to sleep," said Reba.

Katherine sat on the bed beside her and held her hands.

Dr. Stinson asked Katherine, Camila, Betty and Victoria to step into the kitchen for a moment. "Reba only has days to live and you all need to prepare her," he somberly told them.

With tears in their eyes, they all thanked Dr. Stinson as he left the orphanage. Nightfall arrived, and everyone tucked into sleep. Camila shared the news of Reba's worsening health with Nathan and Ethan. They both began crying as they heard and went to bed saddened. Betty shared the news with Jim and he grieved. "I can't believe this is happening to Reba, where are miracles when you need them," Jim cried.

Late into the midnight hour, Reba awakens with weakness and blurred vision. She then heard a creaking sound coming from the living room. "*What is that?*" Reba thought to herself. The sound became louder, "Katherine! Victoria! Wake up! I heard a strange sound in the living room," screeched Reba.

"It's probably an open window Reba, I'll go check," replied Katherine, groggily getting out of bed.

Katherine entered the living room, feeling a sense of calmness. On top of the rocking chair, she saw the glowing eyes of a white dove staring at her. The dove suddenly cooed and the echo seemed infinite. Right after, the dove spread its wings and a hazy, pink figure appeared with a little girl in the center of it. Katherine jumped back in fear as the spirit figure appeared, but then she got angry. "Who are you? Why are you here and what do you want? I'm not afraid of you, ghost. You leave my family and friends alone. Did you place a curse on us?" Katherine questioned, shaking with anger.

"Tell Reba she's coming home soon. Marilyn and Caroline are waiting for her," echoed the spirit. "Why are you doing this? Leave us alone! You and that wicked dove are not welcomed here! You are not taking her or any more of us without a fight. You hear me!" shouted Katherine angrily, grabbing a broom and heading towards the dove.

Suddenly, the dove and the hazy, pink apparition disappeared. Katherine hastily left the living room upset and bewildered as she climbed back into bed alongside Reba.

"Katherine, you seem upset. Are you okay? Were you yelling at someone?" Reba asked in a faint voice.

"No, I'm fine. I just thought I saw something, but it was nothing.

"Oh, okay. I know it sounds strange, but I swear I heard the rocking chair moving back and forth; that chair holds so many fond memories of The Lady in Pink. She was such a loving and caring woman," said Reba as she turned over in bed to go back to sleep.

"Was that truly The Lady in Pink's spirit? And was that child—Reba? No, it couldn't be, I'm just tired, that's all," Katherine thought to herself.

"Goodnight, Reba."

"Goodnight, Katherine."

CHAPTER NINE

KOBE'S HORSE GOES MISSING!

*T*he next day, the men took a walk into town while Betty and Katherine tended to Reba. Victoria and Camila were outside removing weeds of out the flowerbed around the porch.

While tending to the flowerbed, Victoria whispered, "Camila, do you hear a crunching sound?"

"No, a crunching sound?" asked Camila, puzzlingly. The sound of crunching grew louder.

"That!" Victoria loudly stated with wide eyes.

"Yes, I heard it that time," Camila slowly answered. "What do you think that was?" she asked, looking around.

"Sort of sounds like a horse eating," Victoria answered.

"A horse? Here? You have a horse here?" Camila asked, staring at Victoria.

"No, unless The Lady in Pink kept it as a surprise for us," Victoria laughed. They both got up from the flowerbed and looked around. Just then, Victoria heard Camila shriek. "A horse! It's eating my skirt!" The horse was eating grass on the corner side of the house before it took a bite at Camila's skirt.

At the same time, Kobe wildly came running down the road barefooted with a bucket of oats spilling out in one hand and a pair of shoes in the other. Usually immaculately dressed and neatly groomed, Kobe looked out of sorts with his hair ruffled, his shirt untucked and his pants dusty and scuffed at the knee.

"I'm sorry to bother you, Misses," Kobe stated, out of breath, "But have you seen Georgia Boy, my horse, come this way? He took off as I bent down to put on my shoes. Before that, I was trying to feed him these oats. I couldn't get a hold of his reins fast enough before he sped off down the road."

Victoria giggled, looking at Camila's ripped skirt, "Oh, Georgia Boy is his name, is it? Why, yes, Kobe we have been quite acquainted with Mr. Georgia Boy. He is at the back of the house now."

"He's here? Good!" breathed out Kobe, looking relieved.

"Why, yes Kobe, that rascal is definitely here," said Camila. "Apparently, he has a thing for skirts."

"Camila's skirt seems to be his favorite. Aha! Maybe you should lure him with skirts next time," giggled Victoria pointing at Camila.

"Skirts? He was eating her skirt? You said he's at the back of the house?" asked Kobe, still out of breath.

"Last we've seen him," informed Victoria.

"Thank you, kind ladies! I'm very much obliged! Oh, and I'm sorry about the skirt," hastily stated Kobe with a nod as he took off with the bucket of oats dangling from his hands. Minutes later, he appeared from the side of the house walking Georgia Boy, who was snorting and angrily munching oats. "As odd as today has been, it has really brightened the mood around here a bit, don't you think Victoria?" laughed Camila.

Victoria sighed and laughed, "Strangely, it has."

A Gentle Visitor

The moment of laughter was shattered when they heard yelling from inside the house. "Reba! Please wake up, Help!" Katherine shouted hysterically.

Victoria and Camila rushed back inside the house and into Reba's bedroom. Katherine was shaking her and crying, while Betty and Camila are hugging each other and quietly sobbing. Victoria ran outside to find Dr. Stinson while Katherine continued to try waking Reba. Camila and Betty were at Katherine's side trying to help.

Almost an hour later, Victoria came back from town with Dr. Stinson, Nathan, Ethan and Jim. The doctor hurried inside carrying his medical bag and then into Reba's room, the men and Victoria hurried behind the doctor. The doctor began checking Reba, noticing that she was blue in color. Dr. Stinson quietly looked at everyone and shook his head, "I'm sorry everyone," was all he muttered.

Everyone cried as she laid still, smiling peacefully. Dr. Stinson wiped away a tear then gently closed her eyes. Moments later, the white, mysterious dove flew through the bedroom's window and circled above Reba's bed, then gently cooed before taking off. Everyone was dumbfounded by the dove's sudden appearance and exit. Dr. Stinson then quickly left the orphanage to notify Clergy Madison.

When Clergy Madison arrived, he entered the room where Reba was laying. Clergy Madison prayed, "Heavenly father, we approach your throne of peace and ask that you grant us comfort as your daughter, Reba, abide in her new heavenly home. Thank you for the times we all spent together. We will dearly miss her. Amen."

Days later, everyone gathered underneath the Cherry Blossom Tree for Reba's memorial service.

"Look, the tree is dying, four branches have now fallen to the ground!" exclaimed Katherine, in bewilderment.

All at once, Cherry Blossoms began falling and a dove started making a cooing sound as it flew overhead.

Katherine looked up at the dove and wept. She felt powerless and filled with too much sorrow to be angry.

Clergy Madison read a scripture, "And Jesus, when he was baptized, went up straightway out of the water: and, lo, the heavens were opened unto him, and he saw the Spirit of God descending like a dove, and lighting upon him: And a low a voice from heaven, saying, this is my beloved Son, in whom I am well pleased." He then prayed, "Dearly beloved Father, we know that You keep watch over every bird of the air, fish of the sea and creature on land. We trust that you will keep watch over the soul of Reba, our beloved family member. We call her family because we are all a part of your heavenly family. We are comforted that just as Your Spirit descended upon Your Son, your love descended upon Reba. She lived a life of service towards others and showed genuine kindness to everyone. May she find eternal rest, peace and safety in your arms. Amen."

During the service, Katherine held Camila's hand while Victoria held Betty's. Jim stood in between Nathan and Ethan holding their hands. Everyone sprinkled blossoms on the coffin as they passed by paying their respects to Reba's legacy. She was laid to rest next to Caroline, Marilyn and The Lady in Pink gravesites.

Reba's tombstone had her favorite line of poetry engraved, *"With happiness and cheers, I can chase away my fears."*

After the memorial service, Katherine and Victoria carved Reba's name into The Tree and then returned to the orphanage to share a meal.

Katherine took Reba's poetry plate out of the cupboard and placed it alongside Caroline's and Marilyn's plates. Seeing such touching, emotional gestures of love, Betty embraced Camila, Nathan and Ethan with tears. Clergyman Madison and Dr. Stinson both expressed their deepest sympathy before leaving the orphanage.

"Well, we want to thank everyone for their support during Reba's journey as well as our own. We couldn't have made it without each of you," Nathan said in tears.

"We are going to be packing up to leave now," Camila wept.

"Thank you all for helping to take care of my sister," said Ethan with his head down.

They all hugged each other as Reba's adoptive family made their way back to France where the country celebrated Reba's many accomplishments by inducting her into the Sports Hall of Fame in France.

Betty and Jim decided to stay awhile longer to help Victoria and Katherine cope with the loss.

That night, Katherine climbed into Reba's bed, remembering the last conversation that she had with her. She then sat up in bed. Katherine thought that she heard someone crying out early in the morning, "No! Katherine!"

Victoria woke up, crying and shaking. Betty, Jim, and Katherine entered her room to check on her.

"We both heard you yelling through the night. Were you having a nightmare, dear?" asked Betty, deeply concerned.

"Yes, I had a dream and it involved Katherine. But I can only remember something about a dove and cookies. It was so strange, but it felt so real!" said Victoria.

"It was just a dream. It's been a long and painful journey for us all," consoled Katherine.

"Yes, it has," everyone chimed in, agreeing.

"Why don't you get some more rest, dear, and we will prepare breakfast for you in the morning," Katherine said, patting Victoria's hands.

When morning arrived, Betty and Katherine quickly prepared breakfast while Jim delivered trays of food to Victoria's bedroom.

"This smell so good," commented Victoria, fully awakened by the aroma of food. She sat up, smiled and hugged Jim as he placed the tray across her lap. "Thank you, Jim. I am glad you're still here with us. I feel fine now," assured Victoria.

"Caroline wouldn't want it any other way and I was blessed to have you all with us," Jim said.

Katherine and Betty then entered Victoria's room. "I love this poetry plate. It always brings back so many memories of us girls and The Lady in Pink. It's Stillwaters' *modus operandi* for us to say our poetry during breakfast," smiled Victoria. Moments later, everyone noticed Victoria crying while eating her breakfast.

"What's wrong, Victoria? Please tell me you are not feeling sick," worried Katherine.

"No, no, I feel perfectly fine. I'm still thinking about that terrible nightmare with you in it and I can't even remember it. It was just so real," she cried.

"It's going to be alright. That was last night, and this is a new day," stated Katherine in an optimistic tone. She then said, *"As the moon brightens each midnight sky, so does the sun for each tear I cry."*

Victoria stared into Katherine's eyes with a smile and then cited, *"Let peace be still to one and all, no matter how great, no matter how small."*

With their moods lifted, they prayed together and ate their breakfast—richly talking, laughing, and in good spirits. After breakfast, Katherine motioned for Victoria to grab her hand. After Victoria grabbed Katherine's hand, they got up and Katherine led Victoria outside; Jim and Betty followed behind. After going outside and stopping at the tree, Katherine announced, "Now, Victoria and I are going to teach you, Jim and Betty, our Cherry Blossom Tree song that we sang as little girls. It goes like this. *Up and down we go, now hop and touch your toes, skip around the Cherry Blossom Tree, now stop and touch your nose.*"

After repeating the song and skipping around the tree like little children, everyone fell in exhaustion and rested under the Tree. Betty laughed and exclaimed, "I haven't had so much fun since I was a little girl. Thank you for that!"

"This truly tested my endurance. When did I get so old?" Jim said laughing.

Each of them then solemnly stared at the gravesites of The Lady in Pink, Marilyn, Caroline, and Reba. Cherry Blossoms began to fall like teardrops on each of their graves. Katherine slowly walked over to Reba's grave and sprawled on top while weeping. Victoria, Jim and Betty followed, consoling her. After several minutes of crying, Katherine ran inside the orphanage and into Marilyn's room. She then grabbed one of Marilyn's dresses out of her closet.

"I miss you so much! Marilyn, please come back! I'm trying to be strong for everyone, but it's so hard without you," cried Katherine.

Betty, Jim and Victoria followed her into the orphanage later. They stared at Katherine while she rocked on Marilyn's bed, clutching her dress in her hands. They then leaned their heads on Katherine, crying hysterically for all of those whom they missed.

Runaway Carriage

A few days later, Victoria, Katherine, Betty and Jim all decided to go into town as a getaway. As they strolled down the street, Kobe came along singing when he suddenly stopped.

"Good morning, everyone. Can I give you all a ride this fine morning?" he asked.

"Kobe! Good morning, you certainly can! And, good morning to *you*, Georgia Boy! You haven't tried to run away again, have you?" laughed Victoria as she reached up and rubbed Georgia Boy's neck.

"And, no more skirts for breakfast?" chimed in Betty, smiling.

"No, he sure hasn't. He's been a very good boy!" blushed Kobe, while patting Georgia Boy.

"Well, good!" laughed Katherine.

"We're heading into town to shop," said Victoria.

"This is a mighty fine horse you have here, Kobe. Oh, I'm Jim by the way," mentioned Jim.

"Why, thank you, Mr. Jim. He can be quite a handful at times," replied Kobe.

Tears of a Cherry Blossom Tree

They all climbed into the carriage and took in all the beauty of the decorations of Cherry Blossoms that lined the streets and shops for the town's annual Cherry Blossom festival.

"Alright, everyone, we've arrived. Good day, Ladies, and Mr. Jim," said Kobe as he came to a stop.

"And, Good day to you! Thank you, Kobe. And, thank *you*, Georgia Boy. How much do we owe you?" asked Katherine.

"Nothing, it's a courtesy ride for your troubles the other day. Thanks again for helping me find Georgia Boy," replied Kobe.

"Oh, you're very welcome. But, he kind of found us!" laughed Victoria.

On the way to buy some milk at the grocery store, Victoria and Katherine decided to enter the town's bakery to sample a variety of tasty cookies.

"These are so good. I don't want to leave this counter. This is my fourth cookie," said Victoria, licking the crumbs off her lips."

"Yoo Hoo! Yoo Hoo!" yelled the store clerk.

"Yes, ma'am?" answered Victoria.

"Are you all planning to buy something or are you going to just stand there and eat all of my cookies?" frowned the clerk.

"Yes, ma'am, we would love one of each of your cookies," said Victoria sweetly, while covering her mouth to stop from giggling at Katherine making funny faces while eating.

After leaving the store, they all decided to browse the remaining department stores with festivities from the Cherry Blossom in full swing in Macon, Georgia. People were at the event celebrating, enjoying food, music and having fun. After joining in, they all laughed and had a chance to meet people from different areas of town. While they were admiring the various dresses, Victoria looked up and announced, "Look at the town's clock, it's later than I thought and we still haven't bought any milk. We can grab some milk tomorrow, I suppose. We'd better get back home before dark."

They all hoped to catch a ride as they headed for home. However, Kobe was no longer making stops. Knowing the walk would take a while, Victoria and the others started making their way back to the orphanage.

"Let's cross over to the other side of the street and see if another carriage will give us a ride. Maybe someone will stop," suggested Katherine.

"Oh, look at that beautiful dove in the sky. I wish I could fly like one," wished Victoria. She suddenly started twirling about and spreading her arm as though she was a bird.

Katherine frowned her brows as she watched Victoria pretend to be a bird and dance in the street, "Are you mad, Victoria? The way you're acting someone will surely put you in the asylum." Jim and Betty laughed at the hilarious scene.

Victoria still danced around as though she didn't have a care in the world and simply replied to Katherine, "I wish I could *coo* like one, but I can't carry a tune," she chuckled.

"Are you even listening to me, you mad woman?" questioned Katherine as she walked over to Victoria to restrain her. "And I know you can't sing a tune. I've heard you sing, remember? You sound more like a frog's *croak* than a dove's *coo*!" mocked Katherine.

At that, Victoria immediately stopped dancing in street and pretended to be angry at Katherine and threw her white gloves at her. When Katherine tried to dodge the gloves, she accidentally fell backwards on her bottom. They both had a hearty laugh until their sides ached. Jim and Betty were laughing as well.

"You two are definitely sisters," Jim joked.

"I can see why The Lady loved you all so much. There was never a boring moment," Betty said laughing.

After the laughter, Jim helped Katherine off the ground and continued waiting for the streets to clear before crossing. Katherine,

Jim and Betty ran ahead, and Victoria followed. Victoria, hurrying across the road, tripped on the long hem of her dress, causing her to fall to her hands and knees. She looked up at everyone and laughed uncontrollably at herself.

"Just wait right there. I'll be there in second. My favorite necklace and charm fell off somewhere around here," shouted Victoria, still in the middle of the road.

"Well, hurry up and get out of the road, there is a carriage coming," Betty yelled back to Victoria.

While Victoria was on the ground searching for her favorite necklace and charm, an old carriage with two horses quickly started moving towards her.

"Whoa, Whoa, boys!—Whew! You okay, ma'am? It's dangerous to be in the middle of the road like this. I almost couldn't stop these wild horses," said the carriage driver.

"Yes, Yes, I saw you, sir, I am just searching for my necklace," responded Victoria in an irritable tone.

"Victoria! I'm coming to help, so you will get out the road like a mad person," yelled Katherine as she started to walk over to Victoria.

"Hey, lady, you see that shiny thing over yonder? Let me just hop down and…" As soon as the carriage driver jumped down from the carriage to help, he accidentally pulled the reins, causing the wild horse to buck and break free of the old carriage, toppling the carriage onto Victoria as they escape down the road.

"Victoria!" screamed Katherine in shock, dropping her bag of cookies and only feet away from Victoria. Jim and Betty immediately ran to the scene.

"A'right, listen up everyone! Uh, Let's lift it up a bit and you, sir, can gently slide her out from under it," yelled the carriage driver. Everyone agreed to the plan. "A'right, here we go, One! Two! Three, Lift!" directed the driver. They managed to lift the carriage high enough for Jim to slide Victoria from underneath the old carriage wreckage. Victoria was freed, but also unconscious, and covered in blood and dirt from the road. The carriage driver frantically took off to find someone who could help.

"Oh, no! Victoria, open your eyes!" cried Katherine, desperately shaking her.

Onlookers gathered around them and several other people ran from the local shops to see the incident. Jim and Betty kneeled by Katherine, who was now emotionless and staring at Victoria's mangled body. Dr. Stinson, who heard the commotion from his office, ran down the street to where the carriage was overturned and noticed Victoria lying on the ground.

"Get her inside my clinic! Now!" he ordered with urgency to everyone nearby. The onlookers then carefully picked up Victoria and swiftly carried her inside Dr. Stinson's clinic. He tried everything he could medically to revive her, but Victoria never responded.

"We lost her," Dr. Stinson gravely said to Katherine.

Katherine didn't respond to doctor's words, she seemed to be in trance with a blank stare on her face. Then, without saying a word, Katherine walked out of Dr. Stinson's clinic and back into the street where Victoria was struck. She fell to her knees grasping what was left of the cookies while crying and crumbling them in her hands. "Why did you have to look for that wretched necklace? I can't take this anymore!" she screamed up to the sky in agony.

Clergyman Madison chased after her and kneeled alongside Katherine, who was still screaming. "It's going to be alright! We are going to see you through this," consoled Clergyman Madison.

"It's never going to be alright! None of this would have happened if we didn't come to town," Katherine wailed in regret.

"Please, don't do this to yourself. This is not your fault," Dr. Stinson reasoned to Katherine. Suddenly, she remembered the cookies and the dove Victoria mentioned in her dream.

"Victoria thought something was going to happen to me, but it was her all along," Katherine was stunned by the revelation.

"What do you mean?" asked Clergyman Madison.

Katherine explained, "Victoria told us about some dream she had about cookies and the dove, but that's all she could remember." Betty and Jim ran over to Katherine to check on her.

"Here, let me help you up. I will give you all a ride back to the orphanage," offered Clergyman Madison, feeling pity for Katherine.

Katherine rested her head on Jim's shoulder, crying as they made their way to the orphanage in the carriage. When they arrived back to Stillwaters, Clergyman Madison and Jim helped Katherine to the door and into the living room. There, the clergyman began to say a prayer,

"Father, we are trying to make sense of all these terrible circumstances we are encountering. Give us peace and allow us to go through this journey with the comfort of your angels. We know Victoria saw this before it happened. Help us to live through what happened. We miss her so much and our sorrow is heavy. Let your hand of comfort embrace us during this time. Amen." After the prayer, Clergyman Madison hugged everyone before heading back home.

Moments later, Betty and Jim sat with Katherine as she laid helpless, bitterly crying in pain.

Betty exclaimed with red, teary eyes, "Oh, no! We need to get a letter to Victoria's parents. Let me go through her things." Betty located Victoria's adoptive mother's contact information as well as her husband's, Joe.

"Let me get this urgent letter to the carrier as an urgent postage," Jim said.

Katherine sat up and said that she would write the letters to Victoria's family and husband Joe. Betty remained by her side consoling her. When Katherine finished writing the letter, Jim took the letters and ran outside to go to the town's post office.

A little over two weeks later, there was a knock at the door.

"Who's there?" asked Betty.

"It's me, Mrs. Izumi. I'm Victoria's adoptive mother and these are my daughters, Mihoko and Akane," she introduced.

"Oh, please, c'mon in. I'm delighted that you all made it safely. I am so sorry about your loss," Betty said. "Please follow me. I will show you to your room," continued Betty.

As they passed Victoria's room, everyone stopped and entered. Mrs. Izumi and her daughters walked over to embrace Katherine as she laid cradled in bed stricken with depression.

"I know how much you all meant to each other and we will miss her so. My husband died ten years ago. He adored her. I just wanted to thank you and express to you how much I appreciate and love you for what you've done for my sweet Victoria," expressed Mrs. Izumi, dabbing her eyes.

"She was a wonderful person, and I'm glad you and your family were able to make it. I am deeply sorry to hear Mr. Izumi passed. Victoria shared so many wonderful stories of her time with your family, she truly loved you all," whispered Katherine in a faint, raspy voice. Katherine then looked around and asked Mrs. Izumi, "Do you know if her husband received a letter as well?"

"I'm not sure, hopefully, he received the letter. But do not worry, I'll take care of that. Just continue resting and if you need anything you let me know," said Mrs. Izumi with a smile as she exited the room with her daughters. Jim carried their bags to their rooms while Betty settled them.

During their brief stay, Mrs. Izumi and her daughters shared many memories of Victoria becoming an elementary school teacher where Mrs. Izumi once taught.

The next day, there was a knock at the door.

"Who is it?" asked Jim.

"I'm Joe, Victoria's husband."

"Please come in. It's a pleasure to meet you and my name is Jim. Follow me this way." Jim led him into Victoria's room where Betty and Katherine were standing. They all embraced him. Joe began crying as he stared at Victoria's childhood framed sketched picture on the dresser.

"You are welcome to sleep in here if you would like," Katherine said.

"This would be perfect," Joe said.

As the day went on, Joe made his way into the kitchen area where everyone sat to eat. He exchanged stories of how he fell in love with Victoria at first sight. He talked about her as a colleague, friend and wife. As he reminisced, Katherine provided him with a token of memory, Victoria's childhood dress that she wore when she arrived at Stillwaters as a child. "Thank you, thank you, thank you," Joe said while crying and hugging Katherine. Afterwards, everyone ate and went about the rest of the day sharing happy memories of Victoria.

The next day, everyone gathered underneath the Cherry Blossom Tree for Victoria's memorial service. Clergyman Madison prayed, "We look to you Lord when times like these arrive. To everything there is a season, and a time to every purpose under the heaven: A time to be born, and a time to die; a time to plant, and a time to pluck up that which is planted; A time to weep, and a time to laugh; a time to mourn, and a time to dance. Even though we mourn, we know that Victoria is rejoicing in your presence. Despite being absent from the body, we know she is with you. Comfort and give us peace. Amen."

Katherine began giving an emotional speech.

"When we all arrived here at Stillwaters' Orphanage as little girls, The Lady in Pink always made sure we were fed, bathed, clothed and loved. The most valuable things that she ever taught us was how to pray and love one another. Although we arrived with fears, difficulties, and numerous challenges, we overcame our fears together and learned what it meant to be a family. And, despite being separated through adoption, we made it our mission to celebrate and support each other no matter where we were, who we were adopted by or how far we lived. The love we shared here with The Lady in Pink and one another will never be forgotten. Today, as I stand here as the only surviving member of Stillwaters' Orphanage, my heart is heavy with grief. But the joy of knowing that we will all meet again gives me so much comfort. I love and miss you, Victoria."

Her husband, Joe, paid tribute to his wife Victoria, with tears in his eyes, "I will always cherish and remember Victoria as being the most thoughtful and loving wife in the world. I want to thank each of you for your support, love and undying care that you have shown to all us who entered your lives. For that, I will be forever grateful. I will always love you, Victoria."

Mrs. Izumi walked over to Victoria's coffin and paid her respects, "We will never forget the memories of Victoria joining our family. She was our beacon of light and will always be loved. I can never forget taking her to school only to realize that I was imprinting her to walk in my shoes as a teacher. She will never be forgotten. We love you, rest in peace, sweet Victoria." With that, Mrs. Izumi blew a kiss towards Victoria's coffin.

Suddenly, there were loud cooing sounds coming from several doves in the tree and another large branch fell to the ground. Katherine looked up and pondered to herself, "Am I next? Why are you all here? What is your purpose?" She then looked at her last friend's coffin and had a flashback about the funny joke about Victoria's singing right before they had crossed the street on that fateful day. She wiped the tears from her eyes, smiling again at her friend's wonderful sense of humor. Even the Cherry Blossom Tree seemed to cry along with her as its blossoms fell like teardrops while Victoria's coffin lowered into the grave. Everyone reached down to pick up blossoms to sprinkle on Victoria's grave. Her tombstone was engraved with her favorite poetry line; *"Let peace be still to one and all, no matter how great, no matter how small."*

Betty began to sing the hymn, *"I come to the garden alone..."*

The Last Plate

After the service concluded, Mrs. Izumi, her daughters and Joe hugged and said their goodbyes to everyone. They had to rush back to port in order to make their ship's boarding time. Katherine, Jim, and Betty stayed by Victoria's grave for a while and shared fond memories before walking back to the orphanage. After everyone headed back into Stillwaters, Katherine took Victoria's poetry plate out of the cupboard while crying. She placed it next to Reba's, Caroline's, and Marilyn's poetry plates. "There's only one poetry plate left, and it's mine," cried Katherine as she leaned her head on the cupboard.

Betty and Jim wrapped their arms around Katherine with tears in their eyes.

Betty told Katherine, "We can stay here longer if you need us too. We love you."

"Thank you so much, Betty and Jim, for your kind offer and you both mean so much to me, but I would like to be alone for a while and try to figure out my next journey in life. Besides, you two have a life to get back to as well. Time will help heal the pain," said Katherine to Jim and Betty.

"You will always have a place… in our hearts and we are your family, never forget that," said Jim.

"And even though we're leaving today, we will never forget you and the love we found here at Stillwaters' Orphanage. This place will always be special to us and from time to time, we will visit you. You are welcome to visit us as well. Katherine, thank you for the comfort you provided for all us during our journeys here. God will carry you the rest of the way and we will be praying for you." Betty and Jim hugged Katherine, packed and visited Caroline's grave for the last time before starting their travels back to New York.

"They are all gone. It's only me here now," Katherine said to herself, feeling the same familiar loneliness and sadness as on the day her grandmother passed. Katherine left the kitchen and went into The Lady in Pink's room, sitting down on the bed. She stared out of the bedroom window and as the day came to an end, Katherine went to The Lady in Pink's closet and pulled out her pink dress. She then put on the dress and found the last letter The Lady ever wrote. Katherine decided to go and stand underneath the Cherry Blossom Tree near her grave. Katherine stared at The Lady in Pink's last sentence at the bottom of the letter that read:

Katherine, never forget your promise.

With Tears of Love,

The Lady in Pink

Tears of a Cherry Blossom Tree

As Katherine stood holding the letter to her heart, she uttered the words, *"I will keep my promise."* A breeze began blowing as she stared at The Lady in Pink's grave. The majestic stare intensified with a glow on her face and the long flowing pink flowered dress rode on the wind. Blossoms began falling around her. For, in clear view, she saw the familiar sight of the glowing eyes of a glistening, white dove staring into her eyes. Suddenly the dove rested on her shoulder when an intense feeling of peace, love, and comfort resonated inside of her. The dove began to coo and spread its wings. "Dove, I did not understand who or what you were until now. I am sorry. I simply didn't understand." Katherine then stared at that old, Cherry Blossom Tree with all of her Stillwaters family's graves under it and said to the dove, "You are always welcomed here, Dove—and let *them* know that *they* are always welcomed here at Stillwaters as well." Immediately after, the dove loudly cooed and flew away, disappearing into the evening sky.

Stillwaters' Orphanage Home—the once warm, welcoming sanctuary that bore dichotomous mysteries of love and despair, peace, desolation, life, happiness and sadness awakened to a new day. The Cherry Blossom Tree would continue to annually and dutifully bloom for years to come; spreading itself in the spring like a sentinel guarded by a divine luminous white dove that perched in its branches overlooking Stillwaters with its beautiful eyes and calling out with its familiar *Coo!* to anyone who had the inclination to intently hear its divine message of love through *"Divine Dove Calls."*

EPILOGUE

VICTORIA'S CROSSING

[11] He hath made everything beautiful in his time: also he hath set the world in their heart, so that no man can find out the work that God maketh from the beginning to the end (Ecclesiastes 3:11, KJV)

Tears of a Cherry Blossom Tree

There, I saw a bright being with the silhouette of a man covering me with large wings as the carriage fell on top me in the street. Instantly, I knew the being was an angel, he looked down at me and I could almost see his gorgeous facial features through the bright light that encased him. He then picked me up in his arms and carried me through a brilliant, magnificent tunnel of light filled with a thick, swirling, glistening warm fog with rainbow colors piercing through it.

I was momentarily immobilized with fear and a feeling of weightlessness. However, my fear quickly vanished when I heard a soft familiar coo of a dove. Relief and peace immediately washed over me. In the blink of an eye, this being, and I were out of the tunnel that seemed never-ending and in a new place, surrounded by a warm light with clouds. As soon as the angel and I entered this foreign place, the angel put me down on my feet, where my body was suspended in mid-air, and he held my hand. In this place surrounded by light, a beautiful, white dove appeared from out the light and began flying towards me; it left a sparkling trail behind it as it moved, and I found myself staring into the mysterious, glistening eyes of the dove as it neared. It was as though the dove was waiting for me to enter this place. When the dove was only a few inches away from me, it hovered in front of my face. Somehow, I knew and could feel that it had the ability to see right through my soul. Immediately, a feeling of warmth and peace flowed through my entire body. I began crying with this overwhelming sensation of feeling so much love.

Suddenly, I felt a swirling, shimmering wind swish past me. "What was that? And, where was the dove?" I looked down curiously around me to see what was happening then and as soon as I picked my head back up, I saw The Lady in Pink reaching for me. The angel next to me looked at her, then down at me, smiled and vanished. After the angel left, The Lady, not saying a word, smiled and took me by the hand. Next thing I knew, we took flight at an incredible speed together passing galaxies of beautiful, transforming illuminating colors and heavenly lights that sparkled like diamonds. Suddenly, we arrived at the most beautiful, breathtaking scene that I could ever imagine. Plush angel-shaped clouds, lush green rolling hills, singing flowers, crystal clear streams and tall, majestic mountains encompassed the landscape!

All around this new world, I could hear the beautiful, sweet, harmonious voices of angels. I took a deep breath and breathed in the cleanest, purest air that my lungs could ever inhale. Everything was fresh, pure, and clean. It was wondrous. I felt so youthful, vibrant, and alive.

"This can't be real!" I exclaimed to The Lady in Pink, "Can it?"

She laughed and said with a twinkle in her eye, "Yes, my dear, it is very real! And, you just wait! You haven't seen anything yet!" I could clearly see that I was in a new body and felt so youthful. All my senses were heightened, and I could talk by conveying my thoughts. No earthly body could compare to this heavenly body. I could also hear what others were thinking without anyone speaking with their mouths.

And, just as on cue, my father who was killed in a war when I was five years old suddenly appeared out of nowhere and ran to embrace me.

"Welcome home, Victoria!" his voice exuberantly shouted.

My joy nearly exploded! Immediately after, I heard a faint humming noise that slowly grew louder. The louder the humming became, the more familiar it sounded, then I realized that the humming was the same tune of our childhood song from Stillwaters, "*Up and down we go…*" Next, out of a bright gleam of light appeared Caroline, Reba, and Marilyn, who was holding a beautiful baby. All at once, they came to greet me with hugs and kisses. They were all so happy and youthful. Suddenly, on my left and right, stood two enormous angels, standing about nine feet tall beside me wearing brightly lighted robes. I reached over to touch them and the light from their robes clung to my hand, and then I looked down at the greenest grass I've ever seen, also noticing a radiant warm colored light coming from my feet.

"You both are so tall! What are your names?" I asked, amazed by how gigantic they both were.

They both let out enormous, deep laughs that seemed to echo for miles. "Why thank you, Victoria, my name is Goodness," said an angel in with a deep, yet soothing voice.

"I'm Mercy, and we came to escort you to someone who really wants to meet you. Don't worry you will see everyone here again shortly" said the other, in an excited manner.

Instantly, I was in a different area of this new world, alone in front of a *Man in White* with luminosity radiating from His beautiful, youthful face, who was standing in front of a large pearl white gates smiling at me with both his hands out. I briefly noticed there were scars on his palms—it appeared as though something jagged and sharp had brutally torn through the skin, muscles, and bones of his hands. His feet had the same large jagged holes and shined like pure brass. I looked up and refocused on the question that I wanted to ask.

"How did I get here? I was just talking to the giant angels…" I suddenly felt a shock throughout my entire being upon the realization of who I was talking to. "Oh My! Oh My! I can't believe it!

You're *Him*! I know who you are!" I yelled, trembling in amazement and slight fear at the same time. There was a feeling an overwhelming sensation to bow down and worship Him right then and there.

The Man in White said, "Come with me, Victoria," in the most calming voice I've ever heard. I was speechless and could only nod, being in awe of The Man in White. After, my assigned angels appeared next to us, we all walked towards a gate taller than a skyscraper building and completely made out of diamonds and light. "Welcome to Heaven, your eternal home of joy. You can now enjoy the rest of eternity without any sickness, pain or sorrow. I was there when the carriage toppled onto you. I heard your silent prayer and saw your heart of love," replied The Man in White with the most beautiful smile that I've ever seen.

His face shone with an immense brightness as he took me by the hand, leading me through a gate opened by a tall, majestic angel. Everyone followed us inside. There were people of all races and cultures walking together. There was a feeling of love everywhere. My eyes focused on a beautiful Topaz stone water fountain with carvings of white doves, beautiful angels, and mystique fish. The city's architecture looked like jasper stone, clear as crystal.

"Wow! It's so beautiful. The water coming from the fountain looks like it's alive. It's so clear that it looks like pure glass!" I shouted, feeling utterly amazed.

"Please go and drink. It is the Fountain of Living Waters," said The Man in White.

I ran as fast as I could to get a sip of water from this gorgeous fountain. It was the sweetest, most refreshing water I'd ever tasted. The taste buds on my tongue seemed to be jumping for joy with each sip that I took. From the corner of my eye, I noticed little-winged creatures with emerald eyes smiling at me as I drank. Next, I saw a man gliding past me quickly, and then he stopped and circled back around to me smiling and waving.

I smiled and waved back. Suddenly, I felt an overwhelming sense of familiarity. I knew this man. So, I asked him, "Would you mind telling me who you are and how did you get here?"

The man very kindly obliged and said, "I was granted Mercy and Salvation. Right before I died the most brutal death on a wooden cross, a death that I knew I deserved. My Savior and Lord looked over at me and told me that, one day, I would be with Him in *Paradise*."

After the man shared his story, he left at the speed of light. The Man in White and I continued to explore other areas of the magnificent different areas of heaven. Even the way we traveled was extraordinary, we would travel to one part of heaven and in less than a second, The Man in White and I would be in a completely different part of Heaven. One area he took me to was a vast valley, with singing flower gardens. Other areas had Beautiful, vibrant, colorful species of birds and mysterious exotic animals that roamed peacefully and freely everywhere. Many creatures I saw were unfamiliar, some were smaller than my hands and some were bigger than mountains. I also witnessed some creatures that had eyes covering their entire bodies, while others looked like those on earth. However, even those that looked familiar to species on earth were more perfect and distinct in their beauty. I remember encountering one of my favorite species of bird, the peacock. However, this peacock was no ordinary peacock. He had the most beautiful, sleek, midnight-black velvet feathers that I had ever seen. Besides the black velvety distinction of his feathers, his plumage collectively had a bright, vivid hue of vermilion, aquamarine, amber, and sapphire. His long, strong velvety tail was matched in beauty by his elegant neck and regal face. He strutted about very serenely amongst lush, emerald-green foliage that beautifully contrasted the hues of his velvety black feathers.

Beautiful sweet-smelling garden flowers such as violet, pink, and white lilacs and light purplish-blue hyacinths bloomed generously, vibrantly, and fragrantly. The smell of the flowers was so rich, sweet and divine! "Let's go towards the city now, Victoria," said The Man in White, and before I could even blink, we were walking in a new place that had golden gates with diamonds that shone brighter than the stars. I asked The Man in White how it was possible to travel so quickly from one place to another and why it felt as though time has stopped. He told me that time and space were created by God, The Father, and that the rules of time and the limitations of earth doesn't apply to Heaven's spiritual, eternal world. As we entered the gates, the golden city has streets of pure, shiny gold. The mansions had walls built of Jasper stone. Angels were on every corner blowing long golden trumpets as we approached. There were twelve gates with names around the city with angels standing by each gate. There were three gates on the east; three gates on the north; three gates on the south; and three gates on the west. Each of the gates had one pearl. The city was pure gold and decorated with all kinds of precious stones. There was no sun, moon, night or day. The light that came from The Man in White and another unknown source provided light for all of heaven.

There were tall golden mansions with the most luscious green grass swaying to melodic music filling the air. I saw flying creatures and angels with six wings everywhere. There were flowers of all colors singing and swaying along with music coming from above.

"We have been waiting for you, Victoria. Welcome home," said one of the flowers.

"Thank you," I replied in amazement.

The most pleasant fragrances filled the air. Some of the smells came from gardens that were filled with unique spices. There were indescribable colors never seen on earth. I saw beautiful, shimmering white unicorns with mesmerizing, aquamarine blue eyes and long-spanned, elegant wings. There were clear rivers of water that had dolphins splashing and singing. Also, in these waters were even more myriad of animals, some never seen or imagined on earth. There were golden signs pointing the way to an area where pets could be picked up by arriving owners. Lions and lambs were lying in the lush grassy fields beside each other.

As we walked further, I saw children running and playing with angels in the flower gardens. There were no sadness, tears or pain on any faces. Everyone was so happy and joyful. As we walked, I saw words appearing under our feet.

"What are these words?" I smiled and asked The Man in White, who had suddenly appeared again.

"These are the Beatitudes," he gently replied.

As we continued walking along the streets of gold, I saw words slowly appearing after each step; "*Blessed are the poor in spirit, for theirs is the kingdom of heaven.*

Blessed are they who mourn, for they shall be comforted.

Blessed are the meek, for they shall inherit the earth…"

Then, I noticed some of the angels around the city were dancing and joking about. They had street signs in their hands with names written on them. The Man in White smiled at me as we turned right on Love and Mercy Avenue.

"In my Father's house, there are many mansions," He said.

"Where are we going and when will I meet The Father?" I meekly asked.

"Very soon, but I want to show you The Lady in Pink's mansion first," He said.

The Lady in Pink suddenly appeared in front of us and led the way with Caroline following her. I then noticed that different names began appearing along the golden street with each footstep (Reginald, Heather, Nikki, Janie, Billy, and others). "Why are the names appearing?"

The Man in White responded, "These are just a few of the names of residents living in these mansions along this street."

As we approached the outside of The Lady in Pink's beautiful mansion, there were sounds of laughter coming from inside with angels playing with children. Upon entering the mansion, the children all ran to hug us. They were filled with so much love and happiness.

The Man in White laughed and played with them. They all sat on His knee and surrounded Him as He sat around a long table inside of the mansion. The Lady in Pink, Reba, Caroline, and Marilyn all sat down alongside each other, laughing and cheerfully talking. My father and I sat together, joyfully holding hands. Reba and Marilyn sat together, hugging and smiling brightly. Caroline and her mother both sat together, locking arms and glowing with happiness. The children all sat among us smiling. Angels then appeared with the most delicious foods and gently placed them all on the table in front of us.

I prayed, "Lord, bless this food and we thank you for your provision. Amen." I looked up and The Man in White was smiling and staring at me with his brilliant, captivating eyes. "I know that I am in Heaven and *You* are actually here with me, but I still must bow my head to pray, right? I'm quite unfamiliar with the rules here," I sheepishly said.

He, along with everyone else, smiled and laughed.

We all ate scrumptiously, and every delicacy that I ever wanted kept appearing in front of me. After everyone finished their meal, the beautifully decorated dishes the food was served on simply vanished. Several children began climbing in The Man in White's lap, playing in his beard and trying to pull him away to come play with them. He just smiled at them and tossed a small cloud up in the air laughing with them as they chased it. "The Man in White laughed. "Let the little children come to me, and do not hinder them, for the kingdom of heaven belongs to such as these. "Truly I tell you, anyone who will not receive the kingdom of God as a little child will never enter it." Soon after, I heard sounds of little babies coming from another room in The Lady's mansion.

"Where are those sounds coming from," I asked.

The Man in White then said, "Victoria I'm going to show you a moment of the past." The Man in White got up from the table and walked over to me. He placed his hand on my left shoulder, and I was instantly taken back to the time when Marilyn first arrived in heaven. Even though we were in a past moment, it was as though we were actually there in the present time. The Man in White said to me, "Victoria, we are simply observing a piece of Marilyn's journey here. What you are now seeing are only memories and no one in the memories can see or hear us."

We witnessed an angel in the form of a woman appeared and reached for Marilyn's hand when she first arrived at The Lady's in Pink's Mansion. The angel started leading her towards a specific room.

"Where is he taking her?" I asked.

"I had a special gift waiting for her. I am glad you're here to witness such a reunion. Here in heaven, all tears are wiped away," stated The Man in White.

I heard sounds of little babies coming from the room where Marilyn and the angel were about to enter. The Man in White and I walked ahead of Marilyn and the angel and went into the room, and they could neither hear us or see us. We saw The Lady in Pink and a memory version of The Man in White in a heavenly nursery.

"Wait, how are you here with me and also right there in the nursery? Are there two of you?" I asked The Man in White.

He chuckled, "No, there is *only* one of me, Victoria. The version of me you see in the nursery is only a memory of what took place in the past."

"Oh, how marvelous!" I said.

We focused back on the memory and saw The Lady in Pink picking up a little baby boy dressed in a white glowing christening gown. The baby began laughing, happily gurgling and singing, "*Jesus Loves the Little Children.*"

"I love you too, Baby Bo," smiled the memory version of The Man in White, while reaching for the baby.

The baby stared into His eyes with love and touched Him on the cheek. The Man in White playfully kissed his chubby little fingers. He then made funny faces at him and lovingly announced to him that his mother will be arriving soon to pick him up.

Tears of a Cherry Blossom Tree

The baby began bouncing and clapping both of his hands. The Man in White laughed and gently placed him back into his crib. While still being in the memory, The Man in White told me that The Lady in Pink was caring for many babies who died on earth. She was keeping watch over them until their parents arrived. There were women in Heaven by the name of Jennifer, Tabitha, and Amanda rocking the babies.

We then heard a knock at the door. The memory version of The Man in White answered it with a warm, bright smile. An angel stood alongside Marilyn as her escort. "Marilyn, please follow me this way." The Man in White entered the nursery and the same baby reached for Him again. "Your mother has arrived," He joyfully said.

The baby giggled and reached for Marilyn. She leaped for joy embracing her baby with kisses and tears of joy. "It's my Baby Bo! I've missed you so much! I love you!" she shouted with glee. The Man in White stood smiling, and everyone began clapping with joy.

The memory of The Man in White then escorted them both to their mansion. "Grab my hand Victoria, it's time we leave this memory and go back to the present," said The Man in White.

I took his hand and we were immediately back in the present time inside of The Lady in Pink's Mansion. Upon seeing us, The Lady clasped both of my hands in hers and happily announced, "Welcome Home, again, Victoria. How was your trip down memory road! We will get together for praise, worship and Supper soon." She then disappeared out of sight.

"You truly are amazing and do love us. Seeing Marilyn reunite with her baby brings so much joy to my heart," I told The Man in White with a smile.

"Come with Me, Victoria. I have more to show you. By the way, there are no Goodbyes in Heaven." He took me gently by the hand as we left the mansion.

We walked along the golden street when he turned on *Peace Drive*.

"Are we going to another nursery?" I asked, awe-struck by the enormity of Heaven.

"No, I want to show you the mansion I prepared for you and your earthly father."

As we approached the mansion, I saw purple heart-shaped diamonds embedded along the golden walkway entrance. The strongest, most fierce, yet beautiful angels with large, jeweled swords were standing like sentinels at the entrance.

"These are warrior angels who fought alongside fallen soldiers and law enforcement officers on earth," explained The Man in White.

The angels looked down at me with a bright, broad smile. The Man in White then led me towards the back entrance of the mansion, which branched off into a road. As we walked along the road, I saw children happily playing, singing, and eating all kinds of fruit from an exotic tree.

"Can I go and say Hi to them?" I asked, intrigued by this happy scene.

"Sure," He replied, smiling.

As I ran to join the children, I began to feel like I was a little child. I was laughing, giggling, and so happy!

After playing and singing with the children, I took a piece of fruit from the tree. I eagerly bit into it. It tasted amazing. It was so sweet and delicious. "What are your names and how did you all get here?" I finally asked the children after eating the fruit and licking its sweet juice off my fingers.

"My name is Lindsey and I had sickle cell anemia."

"My name is Reginald and angels escorted me here in a chariot. The light that you see around my heart represents love and forgiveness."

"My name is Hunter and I became sick from cancer."

I smiled when I heard Marilyn shouting in a happy, sing-song voice from a distance, "So did I! But cancer will never harm us again, Hunter."

A fourth child then said, "My friends and I were all sitting in our school classroom when we were shot. We felt no pain or hurt. Suddenly, a beautiful glowing stairway appeared, and angels escorted each of us here. We are living with The Lady in Pink until our parents arrive."

Suddenly, a flight of doves came flying overhead in heart-shaped formation cooing a song. I noticed the doves turned back and descended on the luscious grass near a tree. All at once, they changed into angels and spread their wings and started walking towards us.

"Oh my! Look! Did you see that?" I asked the oldest looking child named Reginald.

"Yes, they are the doves that comfort the hurting on earth," he said with a huge grin while strumming the most beautiful music on a golden, harped-type guitar.

"Are you all the same doves that came to Stillwaters' Orphanage that Katherine told me about?" I shouted to a group of angels standing by the tree.

"Yes. I'm the one Katherine threw a bowl at. She sure is a tough one," laughed one of the angels. "We came to introduce ourselves to everyone who went home and to celebrate each one's arrival here," said the second angel.

"We hope you enjoyed the fruit," said the third angel.

"Yes, that was the best fruit I've ever tasted. There's nothing like it on earth. What was this tree called?" I asked.

"The tree is called the Tree of Life," said the fourth angel, munching away at the fruit.

The Man in White came over to hug Reginald and all the other children. He then laughed and played with them. We all picked up sparkling white balls and tossed them to each other. We started gliding, flying and chasing each other with translucent cirrus clouds. It was so much fun. Then, Reginald stopped in the middle of playing and walked over to The Man in White and me.

"I just wanted to say welcome home Victoria before we go. I have a class to teach, and these are all my students. See you around, Victoria," he grinned and looked at the other children. All at once, Reginald and the other children vanished into a beam of light.

"Where did they go?" I asked The Man in White.

He looked at me and said, "To another part of heaven dedicated to technology and science."

"I don't understand," I told The Man in White.

"Learning is very important on earth and it is the same here. Reginald, even as a child, studied and loved science. Even though he wasn't in the physical world long, doesn't mean his skills, knowledge, and passions goes away. God created people to carry out tasks, not only on earth, but in heaven also. Death is often only seen as a tragedy on earth, but it's simply a doorway to another life—not the end of life." The Man in White said as he put his arm around my shoulder. "Are you ready to go, Victoria?" I nodded and then He took me gently by the hand and we began walking down the golden street before turning on to *Compassion Court*.

"Where are we going?" I asked.

"I am going to show you Katherine and her grandmother's mansion," said The Man in White. "Why? Katherine is not here yet," Victoria said.

"She will be here in time," said The Man in White. It still utterly amazed me how when I walked with The Man in White, the natural laws of time, space, gravity, and distance seemed to be irrelevant. We would be present in one place and arrived at another place in mere nanoseconds—in the blink of an eye. We even floated on clouds at times.

As we approached the mansion, Katherine's grandmother began vigorously waving. She welcomed us to view the many rooms that were there. Each room was very distinct with unique styles, various colors and decorative furnishings. There were paintings of Katherine at birth, as a toddler, a young child, a pre-teen, a teenager, and as an adult—all stages of life on earth.

"How do you know what Katherine looks like as an adult? I thought that you died when she was a young child?" I asked her grandmother in awe.

"The angels watch over her from the time she was born. There's also a portal here that allows us to see different events of our loved one's lives while they are on earth. If you look around, you'll notice that each room represents Katherine's journey from earth to heaven." replied her grandmother, smiling.

After glancing through each exquisitely decorated room, I asked, "Why isn't this decorated? There's no decorative furnishings or vivid colors. It's just bright white."

"This room represents Katherine's final journey. I had the purity of Heaven in mind when I left it white, in all its beauty and glory!" smiled grandmother, while clasping Katherine's picture. "She still has work to do on earth. Katherine will be here in time," he said.

"Thank you for the tour," smiled The Man in White as he embraced Katherine's grandmother.

"No, thank *You*!" lovingly stated Katherine's grandmother while looking into the face of The Man in White," I wouldn't be here in this beautiful place if it weren't for You! You sacrificed Your Life for me!"

At that, The Man in White grabbed our hands with His gentle nail-scarred hands and kissed each of us on the top of our foreheads. He looked at me and asked, "Are you ready for another tour?" I smiled and nodded my head. Caroline rushed up to hug me and said excitedly, "I'll see you soon. I'm going to the theme park with Marilyn first!" She winked and disappeared in a flash of light.

"Theme park? There's a theme park here? This place is so amazing!" I blurted to The Man in White.

"Why would there not be a theme park here? All things good, fun, humorous, and joyous originated in Heaven before they existed on earth," He gently explained with a smile. The Man in White led the way and I followed, slowing to admire heaven's beautiful creations. As we continued to stroll by a beautiful green field, we saw a crystal-clear stream of flowing water in the middle of it. I ran to look inside the stream and saw the words floating; *"He leads me beside the still waters and restores my soul."*

"Wow! You've got to see this! This is amazing!" I excitedly shouted, taken aback by all the magnificence and beauty.

The Man in White came over and stood next to me, smiling at my child-like excitement and wonder. Just then, other words began appearing in the stream and fading away; *"The Lord is my shepherd, I shall not want..."*

He gently took my hand, and we continued walking. As a mansion came into view, The Man in White began to slow His pace. We then turned towards the most beautiful mansion that I could have ever seen or could have ever imagined. It was decorated with huge majestic stones of different sizes and colors with prisms of light beaming in all directions. I saw a large welcome sign that had my name engraved in *gold!* and it hung at the entrance of a large long porch. Suddenly, the huge wooden door of the mansion swung open. "Welcome Home!" shouted a large group of people that were inside of the mansion, including the heavenly creatures and beings that were around us.

Then, angels came out of nowhere and escorted me to a long mahogany table where I was seated alongside The Man in White, my family, and other familiar and unfamiliar people. The table was breathtaking and was topped with every kind of fruit, cake, nuts, seeds, and goodies imaginable. I was suddenly overwhelmed with the feeling of love and family.

"Who are these people?" I finally asked, speaking to no one in particular.

"Well, the people you haven't met are your family members who arrived in Heaven before you were born. They are here to celebrate and welcome you home," The Man in White said. At that, tears welled in my eyes. I was truly Home!

After the joyful celebration ended, loud, clear trumpets began to sound. "I must go now. I will see you all soon," said The Man in White. He turned around and walked through the door, vanishing into thin air!

I looked on in utter bewilderment until Caroline happily announced, "Well, let's get ready for The Supper, Victoria! I'll take you to your room to get ready."

My mouth gaped open when I saw the elegant apparel that was waiting for me. It was gorgeously made, tailored with fine, expensive silk and spectacular, rare jewels of emerald, sapphire, rubies, and diamonds. I quickly and effortlessly slid the exquisite flowing white gown over my head. The fabric was so very beautiful, breathable, and soft, it fitted perfectly.

Moments later, I heard glorious singing, trumpets blasting and exuberant worshipping outside the mansion. Elegantly dressed in the finest pure white garment to meet The King for The Royal Supper, all of us who were invited as guests excitedly walked along the streets of gold before turning on to *Joy Lane*. The closer we got to the gathering, we noticed that names began to appear with each step; (*Peter, Andrew, James, John, Mathew, Philip, Thomas, Bartholomew, James, Jude, and Simon*).

"These are names of the disciples that were with Jesus while he was on earth!" I exclaimed.

"Yes!" How exciting!" happily stated Caroline.

"And, look at that tall celestial building made of gold," I marveled and said,

"Look over there! Who are *they*?"

"They are the men and women mentioned in the bible," Caroline chimed in.

"Yes, and that group over there are the disciples. They gather in the halls of knowledge to read manuscripts from the large collection of ancient parchments and to share stories with newcomers. You will meet all of them at The Supper," gently stated a man with a voice so soft and soothing that it was akin to hearing a soft, gentle breeze or being near a relaxing, calming ocean tide. Although His voice was soft and gentle, He had a captivating, commanding presence that immediately drew us to Him. He was dressed in a very fine, pure white silk linen that seemed to illuminate brighter and brighter, gently waving and changing colors with every motion. At intervals, He seemed to disappear and reappear right before our eyes. He looked nearly transparent, like a fine mist, a vapor, an apparition, or—a Spirit. The Holy Spirit! The realization hit me like a ton of bricks! This soft-spoken, gentle entity was the Holy Spirit! As soon as I gathered my wits about who He was, The Holy Spirit blew His gentle, sweet breath towards us. We immediately felt Peace, Comfort, Happiness, Love, and Joy. It reminded me of how I felt in the presence of the mysterious beautiful Dove. The Dove! The Dove that met me out of the tunnel was the Holy Spirit! Now dumbfounded, the Holy Spirit looked at me and said, "Yes, that dove was me, Victoria. I'm only here for The Supper, and also to bring back more power and comfort to those on earth," and with a twinkle in His deep, loving eyes, flashed a bright, beautiful smile, and flew swiftly away in a *Mighty*, colorful whirlwind—leaving behind an echo of a soft coo.

    After such an exhilarating moment of meeting the Holy Spirit. Caroline and I journeyed towards The Supper Hall. "Oh, My! Look at the time, I need to change for The Supper," said Caroline abruptly. She laughed and joked, "Wait—Time doesn't exist here."

Caroline winked and then vanished. Right after she left, The Man in White and Reba appeared by me. The Man in White smiled at me, and we continued to walk to the temple with Reba ahead of us. As we all walked, Reba suddenly stopped when she spied two young men playing and wrestling with lions in a field. "You're going to lose again David!" she yelled. "Not this time Reba, I have help now. Do you want to join in?" shouted back the young man David, struggling to fight off the lions. Reba quickly turned her head back at me, grinned and shook her head. Reba then looked forward at the scene again, "Thank you, David, but I will graciously pass. Besides, I would rather be on the winning team of lions anyways. Have fun!" I was intrigued by how friendly and docile the lions were. "They are like big, playful kittens—not ferocious at all!" I exclaimed. The Man in White smiled at my childlike excitement.

"Yes, that's David and Jonathan. Those two will try to wrestle anything. They will be at The Supper," smiled Reba, adding, "And, in Heaven, all creatures are friendly."

As we continued walking, angels came swishing by on golden chariots of fire, escorting people to The Supper. There were people from all parts of the world walking alongside us, including children. Other women were carrying babies as two women led the way. "Who are the two women?" I asked.

"That's Ruth and Esther. They make sure the babies are cared for during The Supper. I'm going to go talk to them. I'll see you soon, Victoria," Reba said while leaving to go talk to the women. I smiled and waved at Reba as she left and then asked The Man in White. "Are we going into that gold temple with the bright light. Is that where The Supper is being held?" As soon as I finished my sentence, we were instantly inside of the enormous temple, where I noticed a sea of people all dressed in glistening white robes singing, cheering, and dancing around a brilliant being in the distance. "Welcome home Victoria!" All the people and heavenly creatures of the temple greeted me, making me feel so loved, important, and thankful. The Man in White took my hand and said, "Come." Every person and creature in the temple parted, creating a pathway for us to this incredible being that was sitting on a throne, surrounded by giant angelic beings with trumpets. From where we were standing, I could only see a silhouette of a human-like figure moving inside of a thick, blinding, white light. I immediately knew this figure was also the source of light for heaven.

As soon as we walked forward, my entire body started to tremble from the power of this glorious figure. A rainbow circled around the throne and a calm river stream came from it. I also noticed another throne to the right of the bright being's throne, but it was empty. With each step we took, I squeezed The Man in White's hand tighter until we came to a stop, "It's okay Victoria, The Father is The Creator of all you see around you and he loves you," calmly explained The Man in White. "What are those beasts roaming about the throne? They have eyes everywhere, and one of the creatures has the face of a man. I...I don't understand. The clouds, lightning, the fire...The people sitting around the throne. The floating scrolls...How does this all feel so familiar?" I asked in nervousness.

Suddenly, I felt a calmness go throughout my entire body and an urge to move closer to the powerful being. I was intensely drawn to this magnificent entity and without warning, The Man in White and I were at the steps of The Father's throne. Overwhelmed, I kept my head down and tightly closed my eyes as The Man in White began to guide me up the golden steps leading to The Creator. As we slowly went up the stairs, I opened my eyes slightly, right before the white light engulfed us. Still finding it hard to lift my head in the presence of The Father's Glory, The Man in White guided me up one last step and then cheerfully said to the *Almighty* entity, "Father, she's back home." I then lifted my head inch by inch, first seeing the sparkling feet of the royal being. Then, I focused on the majestic robe of The Creator, watching it as it gracefully swayed as though it was alive, moving throughout the entire throne room. Next, I saw The Hands of God, they displayed ultimate power and strength as that of a laborer yet, seemed delicate enough to comfort an infant. As I slowly continued to lift my head, I could literary see a ruby red beam of light through God's chest through the robe. The shine of the light danced like fire and shimmered as precious diamonds in the sunlight, I knew this was the heart of The Father. The beard of The Creator came into my view and was hypnotizing the way it flowed in perfect harmony with God's Being. At that moment, The Man in White caught my attention as he slowly let go of my hand and walked towards the empty throne; it was made out of a beautiful stone and encased with luminous jewels of unique shapes and colors. The throne was also covered with the most intricate hand-carved designs that I had ever seen. When The Man in White reached the throne, he gently sat down and leaned back, displaying ultimate power, royalty, and authority. Engraved on top of the throne's tall backrest were the words (*Jesus, King of Kings*). As I slowly turned my head back to God, a sound unlike any other sound penetrated my very essence. All of the elements of creation and time existed within this sound which I quickly realized to be the Voice of God. The powerful Creator said to me, "Victoria. My child, Welcome home. You have made me proud," I quickly lifted my head and stared into the Brilliant, Face of God, feeling so whole, so complete, so loved—

"Thank you, Father! I'm home—truly Home."

Author's Final Thoughts

Heaven is a place where there is no more sickness, pain, fear, worry, sadness, loneliness, suffering, or loss. It is truly a place of love, joy, peace and happiness forevermore. One day, we will all receive that *Divine Dove's Call*, just as The Lady in Pink and the five orphan girls at Stillwaters. *Will you be ready?* It's my sincere prayer that you will be.

THE LADY IN PINK'S LAST LETTER

To My Wonderful Stillwaters' Daughters

Last night, I had a dream that a Man dressed in White came and took me to the most beautiful place I had ever seen. There were Angels and Doves flying above us as we walked through a colorful flower garden. Also, I saw happy children running and playing everywhere. This place had the most beautiful, peaceful music playing everywhere, and the people in this place seemed so happy. I didn't want to wake up and knew that it was a sign. I'm writing you this letter because I received troublesome news from a Doctor. He told me that my kidneys have failed because of something called diabetes and that I only have a few days left. I have lived a wonderful life but now it's my turn to be adopted... by God. I want all of you to know that my final resting place will be underneath the Cherry Blossom Tree where so many wonderful memories were made. I pray that you girls will always love and take care of one another and never forget the love that I have for each one of you. The back door of the orphanage remains unlock as does the door in my heart for you girls. Every night, I sleep with sketches of you all that I drew and they constantly remind me of our eternal bond. If this letter doesn't reach you before I leave this world, just know that my love will always remain true to each of you.

With Tears of Love,
Your Lady in Pink

Ada Bell Poole's Cherry Blossom Cream Cheese Muffin recipe.

6 cups. flour

2 cups. sugar

3 tbsp. baking powder

1 tsp. cinnamon

1 1/2 cups Milk

6 eggs

1 1/2 cups. butter soft or melted.

2 tsp. almond extract

8 oz. cream cheese softened

5 cups. frozen cherries

sift the flour, sugar, baking powder and cinnamon together.

In a medium bowl, mix together the butter, eggs, milk and almond extract.

stir in the cream cheese and then the cherries

Combine and place in muffin tin liners ¾ full

sprinkle tops with cinnamon sugar and bake at 425 degrees for 15-20 minutes. Let cool and top the muffins with Pink icing and sweet Cherry Blossom shaped confetti

This makes about 36 muffins.

With Tears of Love.

Your Lady in Pink

ABOUT THE AUTHOR

Dr. Fletcher Johnson Jr. is a former police officer, editor, author and educator. He has been married 31 years to his wife, Valerie, and together they have three sons, Jarvis, Christopher, and Joshua. He firmly believes that all who encounter hardships, struggles, pain, and challenges in this life will one day be rewarded with eternal peace, love, happiness, and joy forevermore.

"Ascending to a Higher Calling."

First, thank you so much for purchasing Tears of a Cherry Blossom Tree by Author Fletcher Johnson Jr. We hope you felt inspiration, love, hope, and joy as you read this novel. Once again, thank you so much for your support and we pray for an abundance of health, wealth, love, and happiness in your life. God Bless.

Tears of a Cherry Blossom Tree's *Stage Play* and *Film Production*

Piercing Focus LLC (Publishing and Production Company) is gearing up to turn Divine Dove Calls' novel *Tears of a Cherry Blossom Tree* into a magnificent stage play and film that will spread a message of hope and love to so many people around the world. The team at Piercing Focus is actively **raising donations** to make this dream come true. If you would like to show your **support** and **donate** to these wonderful projects, please visit:

https://www.gofundme.com/tears-of-cherry-blossom-tree-stage-and-film

Piercing Focus LLC and The Author of Divine Dove Calls are so **grateful** for your generosity in supporting this Novel. We will continue our mission of providing hope, love, joy and inspiration around the world.

REFERENCES

- ALSA.org. (2018). *What is ALS?* [online] Available at: http://www.alsa.org/about-als/what-is-als.html [Accessed 17 Aug. 2018].
- My-ms.org. (2018). *MS History.* [online] Available at: https://my-ms.org/ms_history.htm [Accessed 16 Aug. 2018].
- Miles, C. (1913). *I come to the garden alone.* Public Domain. Publishing.
- Rambo, D. (1981). *We Shall Behold Him.* [CD] Universal Music Publishing Group, Capitol Christian Music Group.
- Norworth, J., von Tilzer, A. and Meeker, E. (1908). *Take Me Out To the Ball Game.* [Record] New York: Edison Phonograph Company.
- Woolston, C., Root, G. and Fettke, T. (1977). *Jesus Loves the Little Children.* Capitol CMG Publishing (Integrity Music [DC Cook]) Public Domain.

MARKETING AND ADVERTISING AGENCY / PUBLISHING

www.piercingfocus.com

Tears of a Cherry Blossom Tree

Made in United States
Orlando, FL
06 April 2023